Blaze™

Dear Reader,

I'm thrilled to be back with another book in my latest vampire series for the Harlequin Blaze line! Brent Braddock is the badass of the Braddock Brothers and, of course, one hot-looking cowboy. Once the most ruthless hired gun in Texas, he's now a modern-day bodyguard for the rich and dangerous. He's also wild and reckless and he *never* plays by the rules.

Abigail Trent, on the other hand, has lived every day of her life by a very strict set of rules. As a training commander for an elite special-ops team of navy SEALs, she's had to lose all the "girl stuff" and toughen up in order to claw her way up the career ladder and win the respect of her male peers. While she doesn't regret her choice, she can't help but wonder what it would be like to unleash the wild woman inside her just once.

She soon realizes that once won't be enough, however, when she comes face-to-face with Brent. Abby wants more. She wants forever.

I hope you enjoy the latest in the Braddock Brothers series! I love to hear from readers. You can visit me online at www.kimberlyraye.com or write to me c/o Harlequin Books, 225 Duncan Mill Road, Toronto, Ontario M3B 3K9, Canada.

Much love from deep in the heart!

Kimberly Raye

Kimberly Raye

THE BRADDOCK BOYS: BRENT

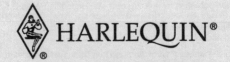

HARLEQUIN®

TORONTO • NEW YORK • LONDON
AMSTERDAM • PARIS • SYDNEY • HAMBURG
STOCKHOLM • ATHENS • TOKYO • MILAN • MADRID
PRAGUE • WARSAW • BUDAPEST • AUCKLAND

Recycling programs
for this product may
not exist in your area.

ISBN-13: 978-0-373-79555-0

THE BRADDOCK BOYS: BRENT

www.eHarlequin.com

Printed in U.S.A.

ABOUT THE AUTHOR

Bestselling author Kimberly Raye started her first novel in high school and has been writing ever since. To date, she's published more than fifty novels, two of them prestigious RITA® Award nominees. She's also been nominated by *RT Book Reviews* for several Reviewers' Choice awards, as well as a career achievement award. Currently she is writing a romantic vampire mystery series for Ballantine Books that is in development with ABC for a television pilot. She also writes steamy contemporary reads for the Harlequin Blaze line. Kim lives deep in the heart of the Texas Hill Country with her very own cowboy, Curt, and their young children. She's an avid reader who loves Diet Dr. Pepper, chocolate, Toby Keith, chocolate, alpha males (*especially* vampires) and chocolate. Kim also loves to hear from readers. You can visit her online at www.kimberlyraye.com.

Books by Kimberly Raye

This book is dedicated to my mother.

Sometimes when life doesn't turn out as planned, the only thing we can do is hang on for the ride.

I know it's been bumpy, but keep hanging on for me, I love you!

1

BRENT BRADDOCK HAD NEVER been the type of man to beat around the bush when it came to something he wanted. He was straightforward. Determined. Persistent.

One hundred and fifty years as a vampire who fed off both blood and sex hadn't changed him much.

While the average bloodsucker tried to curb the lust with a little roll in the hay, Brent preferred going straight for the jugular, no pun intended.

Not that he didn't like sex.

He *loved* it, and he sure as shootin' fired off a round whenever possible. Once upon a time, he'd been one of the fastest guns in the Confederacy and the most precise. Now he called himself a bodyguard and offered his skills to the highest bidder, which meant he spent a great deal of time in the big cities.

New York. Chicago. L.A. Prime hunting ground when it came to getting down and dirty. He could fall into bed with the prettiest filly around and never run the risk of seeing her again.

But this was small town central.

If he bedded a woman tonight, he was sure to bump into her again and again before he said goodbye to this map dot. While she might not remember him thanks to his vamp mojo, he would remember her. Worse, she would become more than a face. And that he didn't like.

He didn't want to know that she'd been voted Most Popular back in high school or that her dad owned the local feed store or that she went to the VFW Hall every Thursday night for spaghetti dinner. He didn't want to know her, period.

Knowing made it harder to turn his back and walk away.

And Brent Braddock *always* walked away.

"I didn't sign up for this," muttered the woman who pushed through the rear Exit of the Dairy Freeze. "I'm a waitress not a bus boy. I do tables, not trash."

The door creaked shut behind her, muffling the whir of a shake machine and the *hisss* and *poppp*! of a burger grill. June bugs bumped against the single bulb that burned near the back door.

She wore a white button up blouse with her name embroidered in pink across the right pocket, white shorts and a pair of white sneakers. Her breaths echoed in his ears and he tuned in to the steady thump of her pulse.

A knife twisted inside of him and his muscles clenched. Heat hummed the length of his spine. His hunger stirred. He watched as she dumped an empty banana crate near the dumpster a few feet away from where he stood in the shadows.

She started to turn, but then her gaze hooked on him and she started. "Holy Toledo," she touched a hand to her chest, "you scared me." She eyed him. "We don't allow customers out back."

"I'm not a customer."

"Then what are you doing here?"

"Waiting." His words slid into her ears and just like that, her annoyance faded and her interest piqued.

Her brow smoothed and her eyes sparked. "For who?"

"Who do you think?" He stared deep into her eyes and tuned into the rush of feelings bombarding her. Her anxiety because she was only one of two carhops on duty on a busy Friday night—the other was old lady Dolly who waited tables about as fast as a Thanksgiving turkey sharpened his own ax. Her anger because she'd spotted her ex, aka The

Rat Bastard, having a banana split with some tramp named Bernice. Her insecurity because she should have remembered to put on a swipe of lipstick before taking out the trash.

Talk about stinking rotten luck.

In the six years since she'd graduated high school, she'd spent a fortune trying every dating service known to mankind only to meet Mr. Tall, Dark and Yummy on her way to the f-ing dumpster.

She licked her lips and tried to think of something witty to say. "Why don't you come around front? I'll bring you one of our new Fat Cow burgers. It's a double decker with bacon and three slices of cheese. It sounds like a heart attack just waiting to happen, but it's really awesome. Especially with our double deluxe strawberry malt—"

"I don't want a hamburger."

"Then what do you want? If it's French fries, I could definitely make that happen—"

"You," he murmured again, but this time he made sure she got his meaning loud and clear. "I want *you.*" He held her stare and willed away everything except the passion bubbling inside her. "Don't talk." He fed her lust with his own until her cheeks flushed. "Don't think." Her breaths quickened. Her eyes sparked. "Just feel."

The clenching inside your body.

The wetness between your legs.
The heat licking at your skin.

He sent the silent messages and her gaze smoldered. Her hands trembled as she stared back up at him, her expression slightly bewildered. Then a light bulb seemed to go off and suddenly she knew exactly what he wanted. Her eyes sparkled as she slid the buttons free on her blouse. The material parted, revealing a white lace bra. She popped the front clasp and pulled the cups apart. Her breasts sprang free. Her nipples pebbled at the instant rush of air.

His gaze fixed on a faint blue vein barely visible beneath her translucent skin. Her heartbeat drummed in his ears, the sound as intoxicating as the ripe smell that spiraled into his nostrils. His gut tightened and his desperation stirred and then everything faded into a sweet red rush.

He leaned her back over his arm, opened his mouth wide and sank his fangs deep into the flesh just to the right of her nipple.

Soft skin cushioned his lips and liquid heat spurted into his mouth. His fangs tingled and his entire body convulsed. He drew on her harder, deeper, her essence tunneling down his throat and warming him from the inside out. She trembled and gasped and he knew she felt the pleasure as keenly as he did.

The satisfaction.

It rolled through him after several delicious seconds and the tightness clenching his muscles started to ease. The fist in his gut loosened and suddenly he didn't hurt so much.

He indulged for a few delicious seconds before sanity sent up a red flag and a loud *Enough*! The beast was sated.

For now.

Easing the pressure, he retracted his fangs. He licked the tiny prick points, savoring the last few drops before leaning back. He caught her gaze and willed her to forget everything.

No tall, dark cowboy lurking in the alley behind the Dairy Freeze.

No uncontrollable lust urging her to strip down.

No fangs sinking into her breast.

Nothing but a sweet, intoxicating orgasm brought on by a very delicious daydream.

He pulled her blouse together. His fingertips lingered at one ripe nipple before he pulled away, buttoned her up and sent her back inside to finish her shift.

After that, he turned on his heel and did what he'd been doing for the past century and a half, ever since he'd been turned into a vampire on that fateful night so long ago—Brent Braddock walked away and never looked back.

2

"WHAT CAN I DO you for, sugar?" asked an ancient woman wearing a white button-up blouse, white polyester slacks and a pink apron.

"I'll have a double chocolate malt." Abigail Trent gave the hand-held plastic menu another once-over. "With extra whipped cream."

Dolly—according to the name embroidered in hot pink on her left pocket—pushed up her cat's eye glasses. "You sure about that?" She gave a pointed stare at Abigail's plain black combat boots before shifting up, over a pair of worn Levis, to her *Go Navy* hoodie. "We've got some nice fruit smoothies, sugar. Why don't you have one of those?" The old woman winked. "Half the calories."

Abby ignored the pinch to her ego and held tight to her resolve. "I'd rather have a malt."

Dolly wiggled her carefully penciled in eyebrows as if she were about to dangle a carrot. "We've got fresh mango banana."

"I don't like bananas."

"Strawberry Kiwi."

"I don't like kiwi."

Dolly gave her another once over. "You know, sugar, you're not half bad. What I can see, that is. If I were you, I'd definitely lose that there Unibomber look you got goin' for yourself. Especially if you want to rope a cowboy."

Abby narrowed her gaze at the presumptuous woman. "Do I know you?"

"The name's Dolly Cook and the real question is, do *I* know *you*?" She waved a crippled hand. "See, I know everybody in this town. Been working here for the past forty-eight years since me and my husband opened up the place. He passed on about five years ago, God rest his soul. My son took over the kitchen on account of the arthritis in my hands makes it impossible to grip a spatula. Luckily, it ain't spread to my feet and I can still walk up a storm." She indicated the white orthopedic shoes that she wore. "I handle the tables on account of I have a crackerjack memory and don't need to write anything down." She narrowed her gaze. "I ain't never seen you here before. You're new in town." Dolly arched a white brow. "Visiting family?" Abigail shook her head and the old woman added, "Looking for a job?"

Abby shook her head. "A person."

"Just what I thought." She waved a hand. "We get it all the time, what with the divorce rate sky high and the number of good men dropping faster than the stock market on a bad day. Why, women drive in from at least a dozen counties to scope out the local pickins. It's closer than driving to San Antonio or Austin and there's a lot less traffic, lemme tell ya."

"I'm not here looking for—"

"'Course when they realize the women around here are just as desperate," she went on before Abby could finish, "they usually end up heading for the city. Take that group over there." She let her gaze shift to a nearby table full of women nursing glasses of pink froth. "They'll load up on strawberry smoothies and then head for the honky tonk out on Route 9. When they strike out there—and they will strike out on account of every man this side of the Guadalupe will be over at the VFW for poker night—they'll head for Austin. They might have better luck there, but I wouldn't put my money on it. A good man is hard to find these days." Her gaze shifted back to Abby. "Sugar, if you want to lasso yourself a decent cowboy, you need to give yourself every advantage. That means ditching the fatty malt."

"I'm not trying to lasso a cowboy."

"Sugar, you can deny it all you want. But I see what's right in front of me. You've got desperate, hopeful and horny written all over your face. You're looking for a man, all right."

Yeah, she was. But it wasn't what Dolly thought.

Command Master Chief Petty Officer Abigail Trent wasn't looking for just any man. She was hot on the trail of *her* man, aka Rayne Montana, the best of an elite group of Navy Seals that Abby had hand-picked and trained herself. He'd gone AWOL two weeks ago in the mountains outside of Afghanistan.

Her first thought was that he'd gotten himself killed. But they'd yet to recover a body. If he'd been kidnapped (her second thought), his abductors would have contacted the Navy to bargain a trade for one of their own by now.

The MPs had come to the conclusion that he'd snapped from the pressure and bailed. They were in the process of tracking a credit card trail from Afghanistan to Switzerland.

But Rayne was too smart to leave such obvious clues. Even more, he was too good to cut and run. Too loyal. Too trustworthy. Like Abby, he'd been career military. Married to his job. Proud of each and every operation. He took his duty seriously. He wouldn't have abandoned a mission and compromised his entire unit unless he'd had no other choice.

Unless he was in serious trouble.

Despite what the higher ups were saying.

They were blaming Abby. They were convinced he'd cracked and that she'd been remiss and failed to notice. She'd been the Officer in Charge. The sole person responsible for the success of the mission and the safety of each man involved. It had been her duty to bring everyone home. To account for each and every man in her unit.

And that's what she intended to do.

Abby had let the MPs go on their wild goose chase while she'd taken a two week leave and hopped a plane for Rayne's hometown. It was Psych 101. When people were scared, they often gravitated back to the familiar. And if there was one thing Abby knew, Rayne Montana had to be scared. Fear was the only thing that would have pulled him away from the military.

And kept him away.

At least that was her latest theory and the one that had brought her to Skull Creek, Texas, to see if maybe, just maybe she could find a clue as to his whereabouts. Maybe he'd reached out to an old friend. Called them up. Paid them a visit. Sent them a letter. An e-mail. A text. *Something*.

She'd driven into town just a half hour ago and now she was here at the local drive-in, the only place open past sundown on a Friday night.

Located on the outskirts of town, the Dairy Freeze was the quintessential small town scene and the exact opposite of the various cities where her father had been stationed while she'd been growing up. Twelve of them to be exact, in as many years. He'd been a leading Naval recruitment officer back then, a job that had demanded constant travel and so they'd moved regularly. But while the address had changed, the atmosphere hadn't. Crowded. Noisy. Impersonal.

This place was crowded and noisy, too, but it was different. People knew each other. They smiled. They talked. Her gaze shifted to the cluster of round wrought iron tables that sat in front of a sliding order-up window. At one table, a busy mother handed out ice cream cones to a group of messy youngsters. At the next, an elderly couple drank root beer floats, shared an order of onion rings and offered up a stack of napkins when one of the kids dumped his ice cream in his lap. Next to them a cluster of teen-age boys in high school letter jackets and cowboy boots mingled with a handful of girls from a nearby car. Rows of drive-up stalls, filled with everything from pick-up trucks to mini-vans, lined either side of the busy courtyard area. People rolled down their windows and chatted with whoever sat next to them while the latest George Strait song drifted from the outdoor speakers. The smell of chili cheese fries and sugary sweet soft serve filled the air and stirred a strange sense of longing.

For food, of course.

Abigail had been living on powdered milk and beef jerky in the mountains outside of Kabul for the past six months. She certainly wasn't feeling suddenly hollow because the entire scene reminded her of her late mother and the one visit she'd paid to her grandparents when she'd been five.

She pushed aside the strange sense of melancholy and steeled herself as she faced Dolly.

"Thanks for the advice, but I'd rather have the malt." Words to live by as far as Abigail was concerned. Men were distracting. She'd learned that firsthand back in high school when she'd almost thrown away a full ride to the Naval Academy for one measly date with the captain of the hockey team. She'd lusted after him for months, dreamt about him, penciled his name on her notebook. He'd been so perfect and she'd wanted him so much. Enough to miss her application interview in favor of getting her hair done for the first—and only—time to try to impress him.

A wasted effort because the Hockey Hunk had stood her up for the head cheerleader. A girl who wore short skirts and high heels and lots of makeup. Luckily Abby had had a perfect record and so the acceptance board had rescheduled her interview and given her one more chance.

She'd realized then and there that she simply couldn't compete when it came to all the girlie stuff. Her hair would never curl quite as much and her body didn't fill out the sexy clothes quite as well. She'd also vowed to never let a man make a fool of her ever again. While she went out every now and then (she was a grown woman with needs, after all), she didn't let herself get emotionally involved. She didn't sit around dreaming of a big wedding or a happily ever after. She was living her dream—to stand on her own feet, command her own unit and serve her country.

She was good at it. She liked it. Even if it was a little lonely every now and then.

"Oh, and add a double chili dog to that," she added, eager to ignore the sudden tightening in her gut. Real food hadn't been the only thing she'd done without all those months in Afghanistan. It had been over eleven since she'd been with a man and she needed a really good orgasm in a really bad way. Not that a man was required in order to have one, but vibrators had yet to become standard issue special ops gear and so she'd been forced to leave her deluxe model Big Man at home. Since she didn't fraternize with her men and in-field operations didn't permit time or energy for fooling around, she'd done without. Add the fact that Rayne was missing, and her superiors were holding her personally responsible to the mix, and she was definitely feeling some major frustration.

"Add a double order of chili cheese fries to that, too," she told Dolly.

"Whatever you say." The old woman pursed her lips. "Damned young folks. Never listen to one iota of advice." She turned and waddled toward the glass door that led inside.

"With extra cheese," Abigail called after her before turning her attention to her surroundings.

She wasn't asking any questions yet. She'd come off a hellacious flight and she was tired. Which meant that tonight was all about doing a little recon and memorizing the lay of the land while she ate her first decent meal in ages. Then she would check into the nearest motel, plan her strategy for tomorrow's Q & A and get a good night's rest in a real bed.

She did a quick visual assessment, noting the faces and the cars and the details. She was good with details. It was one thing that made her a top notch commanding officer. That, and her instincts. She could assess a situation in the blink of an eye and note any threats, and then she could take the appropriate action. Deploy. Advance. Flank.

Run!

The warning echoed the moment she spotted the cowboy who rounded the side of the building. He made his way toward a beat-up 1967 Chevy Camaro parked near the road.

A pair of black jeans outlined his long, muscular legs. A black button-down shirt, the tails un-tucked, framed his broad shoulders. His sleeves were rolled up to his elbows to reveal the detailed image of a six shooter that had been tattooed on the inside of his left forearm. He wore a black Stetson tipped low on his head, shrouding the upper part of his face.

While he fit with the locals—he certainly looked the part with his boots and Stetson—he didn't *fit*.

She tried to picture him swapping stories at the local feed store or hanging out here at the Dairy Freeze, and she couldn't. His entire persona seemed much too intense, too detached, too mysterious for a small town like Skull Creek.

Too sexy.

The thought struck as her gaze hooked on his sensual mouth. An unexpected visual struck—of that mouth pressed to her throat—and her nipples snapped to attention. Need sliced through her, sharp and swift, and her stomach hollowed out.

As if he sensed her reaction, he turned. He tipped the brim of his hat back and the light illuminated his high cheekbones and sculpted nose. A fierce green gaze blazed across the distance between them and collided with hers.

Her breath caught and her heart paused. It was a crazy reaction for a soldier who made it her business to feel nothing and stay focused.

But for the next few, frantic heartbeats, her brain seemed to scramble and she forgot everything except him and the way he looked at her. Into her. As if he could see past the thick outer exterior, to the soft, vulnerable woman beneath.

As if that woman even existed.

She didn't.

Abigail had accepted that fact a long time ago when she'd failed so miserably with Hockey Hunk. Three hours in Chicago's top salon hadn't been enough to transform her from a pudgy tomboy into a desirable woman.

She'd still been too stocky, too shapeless, too ballsy.

Then and now.

But that was okay. She was a commanding officer, not a Hooters girl. She didn't need that kind of superficial attention. She needed respect.

Well, that and a really rocking orgasm to ease her current nerves.

His gaze swept her from head to toe and stripped away every scrap of clothing. Anticipation zapped her and the air bolted from her lungs.

He grinned then and she had the unnerving thought that he knew her frustration. That he knew *her*.

She stiffened and put up the invisible barricade vital to a special ops soldier. No expression. No emotion. Nothing. Just name, rank and serial number.

His gaze widened and surprise flashed in the bright green depths. At least she thought it was surprise. But then he turned, the car door opened and he disappeared inside. The engine caught.

A rush of panic bolted through her and she pushed to her feet.

Because Abigal Trent didn't waste her time thinking and analyzing. She was a field operative. Paid to trust her gut and act on it. And her gut told her something wasn't right.

He wasn't right.

He was hiding something, and there was only one way to find out exactly what that was, and whether or not it had anything to do with her latest mission. There was always the possibility and with her reputation hanging in the balance, she wasn't leaving any stone unturned.

Abby headed for her rental car and took off after him.

3

SHE WAS FOLLOWING HIM.

He knew it even before he saw the blaze of head-lights in his rearview mirror. He felt her. He'd felt her the first moment she'd spotted him.

Her piqued interest. Her pulse-pounding lust. Her surprise. She'd never reacted so fast, so fierce to any member of the opposite sex and it had freaked her out.

He knew the feeling.

It didn't matter that he'd sucked down enough blood to last him several days. His gaze had met hers and bam, the hunger had sliced through him, cutting him to the quick and scattering his common sense. In an instant, he'd wanted to forget everything—partic-ularly the all-important fact that his youngest brother Cody was waiting for him, along with the computer genius that was going to help him track down his sister-in-law. That's why he was still stuck in this hole-in-the-wall. He needed a lead on Rose and her whereabouts. Once he had enough information, he would hit the road and find her. After he watched his youngest brother tie the knot next week, that is.

Then he would uncover the truth behind the tragedy that destroyed his family and his home one hundred and fifty years ago.

He could still see the flames on that fateful night. Smell the sharp scent of smoke and decay and death.

The Braddock Boys had ridden into the chaos together. Brothers who'd vowed to watch out for each other. A pact they'd made as kids when their father had abandoned them to ride off after some saloon whore. Lyle Braddock had died in a bar fight not long after, and not one of his boys had mourned him. They'd been too busy taking care of each other to worry over the no-good sonofabitch and the fact that he'd never been much of a father figure.

When Cody had up and left to join the Confederate cause, Brent and his brothers had ridden along to keep an eye on him. They'd seized supplies and helped Confederate troops and made a name for themselves as the most notorious raiding group the Union army had ever seen. They'd sure-as-shootin' been a major pain-in-the-ass to Quantrill and his boys.

But then the war had ended, the South had lost, and the Braddocks had headed home.

They'd arrived to find the entire ranch—the main house, the barn, the outbuildings—consumed by flames. The herd had been scattered. And what was left of his family? Gone.

Dead.

A nightmare. That's what Brent had thought as he'd leapt off his horse and tried to save what he could, who he could. The whole scene had seemed so surreal. The dead bodies, most burned beyond recognition, stretched out here and there——his mother, the half dozen hired hands, the ranch foreman, Colton's wife Rose, their six year-old son. But then reality had hit along with a very real crack to the back of his skull. He and his brothers had been attacked from behind, each picked off one-by-one, and left to die.

They would have been six feet under for sure if not for Garret Sawyer. Garret was the creative genius behind Skull Creek Choppers, the fastest growing custom motorcycle manufacturer in the South. He was also the two hundred year old vampire who'd turned the Braddock Brothers that night and given them a second chance at life.

At vengeance.

Up until two weeks ago, Brent and the rest of the Braddocks had blamed Garret for the massacre. They'd been hellbent on finding him and doling out justice. Cody had been the lucky one who'd tracked him to Skull Creek first. Only, it had turned out that Garret had been innocent. He'd arrived after the attack and done all he could to save the brothers who'd been just this side of death. Garret had given them his blood and brought them over in the nick of time, but he'd been too late to save anyone else. Or so they'd thought. But Garret had revealed that he'd also turned a wounded couple he'd found several miles away. The vampire had assumed they were victims of an Indian attack and so he'd done what he could to help—he'd given them his blood the moment they'd taken their last breaths.

A man and a woman.

Rose.

After all this time, she was still alive. Still out there somewhere. A vampire.

While Brent had no idea what had happened that night—if she'd been an innocent victim or a cold, calculated murderess who'd orchestrated the massacre and sacrificed her own son—or who the man was that had been with her, he knew that she knew.

She held all the answers and he wouldn't stop until he'd found her.

All the more reason to forget the damned ache in his gut, hit the gas and lose the woman trailing him.

Cody was waiting.

Even more, Dillon Cash was waiting. Dillon was the one doing the research on Rose, compiling information and trying to come up with a lead. He needed to get his ass in gear and head over to Dillon's.

At the same time, he couldn't shake the curiosity that churned inside him. Particularly since he had no clue who the woman was or what she wanted from him.

Nothing. Nada. Zip.

Which didn't make a damned bit of sense because he was a friggin' *vampire*. When it came to the opposite sex, he read every thought, anticipated every move. There were no surprises.

Until now.

Until her.

Sure, he'd connected with her initially like he did with all humans. He'd seen her initial reaction—the surprise, the lust, the longing. But then her expression had closed like a window slamming shut and he hadn't been able to pick up anything else.

No name.

No background.

No intentions.

One hundred and fifty years and he'd *always* been able to read a woman's thoughts. But damned if this one hadn't shut him out. A fact that made him almost as hard as the lusty beast that lived and breathed inside of him.

He was intrigued. Aroused. Hungry.

And while the last thing Brent needed to do was waste his time with confrontations, suddenly it was the only thing he wanted to do.

He eased off the gas, pulled onto the side of the road and climbed out of the car.

This was not good.

The warning screamed in Abigail's head the minute she pulled up behind the Camaro.

Her headlights sliced through the darkness, illuminating the abandoned car. Her gaze shifted to the pastureland that stretched for miles on either side of the road. He was nowhere in sight. No shadowy figure fleeing in the moonlight or trucking down the road. Which meant that while the car appeared abandoned, it wasn't.

Fear made her heart pump faster and she drew on it. Despite what most people thought, fear could be good. It motivated people, kept their senses heightened and sharp. Most of all, it fed the survival instinct. The key was not to let fear get the upper hand and interfere with brain function. It was all about breathing and thinking. Abigail had learned that during her first special ops mission in Iraq. She'd been cornered by a small group of insurgents who would have captured her had she given in to the gripping terror in the pit of her stomach. The visions of interrogation and torture and death. But instead of the outcome, she'd focused on the moment. On thinking of a way to get to the knife in her boot. Plotting a line of attack. Finding a means of escape.

The fear had turned to power then and she'd made it out alive.

She forced another deep breath and stared at the car in front of her, her gaze searching for some sign that he was still in it. He had to be.

Her gut tightened, her instincts screaming yet again that something wasn't right. Why would he hide unless he had something to hide? She killed her engine, leaving the headlights blazing, and climbed from behind the wheel.

A few seconds later, she eased up beside the car, every nerve in her body on high alert as she slid along the sleek finish and stalled just shy of the door. Her gaze sliced to the right, through the window and the thick darkness to find…

Nothing.

He wasn't sprawled on the front seat or hunkered in the miniscule space in the back.

The Camaro was empty.

Impossible.

She whirled, drinking in the surrounding countryside. She'd been all of twenty seconds behind him. No way could he have crossed the wide open pasture in that short amount of time. Not flat out running. Not even hauling it on a four-wheeler.

Her mind raced as her attention shifted back to the muscle car. Her gaze dropped to the foot of space between the bottom of the car and the ground. It wasn't enough to accommodate a man of his size. At the same time, she'd seen seven men stuff themselves into a crawlspace the size of a single shower stall to escape capture. Desperation was the mother of the impossible.

"You might as well come out." Abigail summoned her most commanding voice. "I know you're under there."

"Actually," the deep, timbre of his voice slithered into her ear a heartbeat before she felt his presence, "I'm out here." A hand touched her shoulder. "Right behind you."

4

SHE WHIRLED AND STARED up at him with blue eyes so clear and vivid that he should have been able to see everything going on in her head. She was startled. That's all he got before the window slammed shut and he was pushed out.

For the first time, he found himself stuck noticing her features. The sparkle of her eyes. The fullness of her cheeks. The smattering of freckles on the bridge of her nose.

Cute.

But Brent didn't do cute. Even more, he didn't do locals. So what if she had the bluest eyes he'd ever seen and a pink, pouty mouth that inspired the most wicked thoughts? He wasn't interested. No sir.

Her lips parted and the faintest intake of breath echoed in his super sensitive ears.

The sound echoed in his head, rumbled down his spine and made a bee-line straight to his cock.

Okay, so he *was* interested. But he knew it wasn't the lust that drew him. He couldn't help but wonder what was going on behind her closed expression, and how she managed it in the first place. No woman had ever shut him out before.

Except his new sister-in-law, that is. But Brent had always figured that had something to do with the fact that she'd been sucking face with his brother. She and Cody had exchanged blood and so she shared his strength. Translation? She wasn't susceptible to another vampire's influence.

But this woman didn't draw her strength from another bloodsucker. It was all her own and damned if that fact didn't turn him on in a major way.

She hadn't had sex in a really long time.

It wasn't a truth he read in her gaze. Rather one that he gauged in her reaction. The stiffening of her body, the rapid in and out of her breaths, the frantic pulse beating at the base of her neck.

He stiffened. "Why are you following me?"

"Don't flatter yourself. I was taking a drive and I saw your car on the side of the road. I thought you might have broken down."

"I saw you back at the Dairy Freeze."

"I like to drive after I eat. It helps the digestion."

She killed the eye contact and cast a glance at his car. "So what's up?" She rounded the front end and started to lift the hood. "Did you overheat?"

He rested a hand atop the metal and pushed it back down with a loud *whackkkk!* "You're good."

"What's that supposed to mean?"

"You don't even blink."

"I'm afraid I don't know what you're talking about."

"You're feeding me a load of bullshit and most people blink when they do that. But you haven't batted an eye."

"Maybe that's because I'm not lying."

"Or maybe," he rounded the car and stepped up to her, "you're just really, really good at it."

Abby had the sudden urge to step back. He was too close and he smelled too good and she was too freaked out by both. Particularly since she didn't get freaked out. Ever. She kept her cool. Her focus. Her objective. Always.

Until now.

Until him.

"What are you really doing out here?" His deep voice slid into her ears and made her heart beat that much faster.

Her hands trembled and she stiffened, determined

to get a grip and keep her mind on her mission. "I'm looking for a man."

He regarded her for a few frantic heartbeats before a grin tugged at the corner of his mouth. "That much I can help you with." His meaning hit and a wave of heat swept through her.

"That's not what I meant." She licked her suddenly dry lips. "I'm looking for a specific man."

"For a specific purpose?" He arched an eyebrow and her heart paused. He was playing with her. She could see it in his eyes and hear it in the deep timbre of his voice. "I'm a jack of all trades. Maybe I can help you out."

Yeah, baby.

She ignored the frantic cry of her hormones and tried to remember the details of the story she'd worked out on the drive from San Antonio to Skull Creek. "I'm looking for my ex-boyfriend. We broke up last month and he moved back here. I think." She didn't sound half as convincing, but then that was the point. To play the sad, confused, pathetic ex-girlfriend and get the locals to talk to her. "One of his relatives passed on and left him quite a bit of money but the estate lawyer can't seem to locate him."

Something sparked in his gaze. "So you're not from here?"

She shook her head. "I've got a place in Chicago, but I don't see it much. My job keeps me busy."

Sales. That's what she was going to say when he asked what she did for a living. She'd been through enough interrogations to know that that was the next logical question.

"So what is it you're after? A piece of the money, or do you still have a thing for him?"

"Sales."

"Excuse me?"

Yeah, excuse me? Let him ask the question before you answer, dumbass. What are you thinking?

But she wasn't thinking. Standing there, with the moonlight spilling down around them and his scent filling her nostrils, the only thing she could do was feel. The sweat trickling between her shoulder blades. The awareness rippling up and down her spine. The hollowness between her legs.

"That's what I do for a living," she blurted. "In case you were wondering."

"I wasn't. So are you going to answer the question? Money? Revenge? Which is it?"

"Closure. Our break-up was really abrupt. He moved out with no warning and the only thing I got was a text message saying goodbye. I figured if I came here to tell him about the inheritance, it would give us a chance to talk about things." When he gave her a doubtful look, she added, "You wouldn't under-stand. It's a girl thing." Or so she'd heard. She'd never been much of a "girl". Not in the way she acted—no strutting her stuff or wowing men or texting her BFF about her latest conquest—and certainly not in the way she looked—no skimpy clothes or make-up or lacey panties. That truth had always been something she'd been proud of.

But staring up into his gaze, she found herself wishing she'd put on something—anything—besides baggy jeans and a hoodie.

"So what's his name?"

"Who?"

"The ex-boyfriend?"

"Rayne." She stared deep into his eyes, searching for some spark of recognition. "Rayne Montana. Do you know him?"

"Can't say that I do. I'm just passing through my-self. I'm visiting my brother and his wife. In fact," he glanced at his watch, "I'm running late. I was supposed to meet them fifteen minutes ago."

She tried to ignore the sudden disappointment that washed through her. "Sorry about the misunderstand-ing." She started to dart past him, but he caught her arm before he could think better of it.

His fingertips seemed to tingle, sending shock

waves through her. Her stomach hollowed out and her nipples pebbled.

"No bother." His gaze pushed into hers. "So what does he look like?"

She glanced up from the point of contact. "Who?"

"The boyfriend."

"Ex-boyfriend." She wasn't sure why she felt the need to correct him except that she'd always been a stickler for facts. It certainly had nothing to do with the fact that she didn't want him to think she was actually attached. As if he'd even be interested.

But that was the thing. Despite her hoodie and baggy jeans and regulation cotton underpants, he did look interested. His gaze gleamed with a dozen wicked thoughts and she couldn't help herself.

"We're not together anymore."

"I sort of figured that's what *ex* meant."

"He's a little over six feet," she rushed on, eager to ignore the heat creeping into her cheeks. Blushing? She didn't blush. She didn't stammer. She didn't act like a freakin' idiot. "Short, dark hair. Very fit. Scar on his left bicep."

"If I see anyone that fits the description, I'll send them your way. By the way, what's your name?"

"Abby. Abby Trent. Yours?"

"Brent Braddock."

"Nice to meet you, Brent."

"My pleasure."

The last word conjured all sorts of images as Abby climbed into her car and headed back to the Skull Creek Inn, and straight into a cold shower.

Because the last thing Abby intended was to get side-tracked by a man. She had a job to do and she fully intended to stay on course.

No matter how much she suddenly wanted to take the nearest Exit to Sexville.

5

"I'D ALMOST GIVEN UP on you," Cody said when Brent finally walked into *Mary Sue's Wedding Nirvana. Mary Sue's* was the one and only bridal shop and tuxedo rental in Skull Creek and the last place Brent wanted to be at the moment.

His pulse pounded and his muscles clenched. He was wired. Desperate. Hungry.

"You were supposed to be here a half hour ago." Cody stood to the left near a small sitting area. He worked at the buttons on his white tuxedo shirt. "All the other guys have gone and left."

"Sorry to miss the party but I had something I had to deal with." Brent sank down into one of the leather chairs and tried to ignore his brother's curious gaze.

Cody arched an eyebrow. "Something or some-one?"

"Does it matter?"

"No, it's just that you might want to watch yourself around here. It's a small town. A safe town. The last thing we need are rumors flying." He finished the buttons and shrugged on the black jacket. He turned towards Brent. "What do you think?"

"I'm glad you're the one getting married and not me."

"It's not so bad." He flexed and the fabric pulled and tugged. "Granted it's not nearly as comfortable as a T-shirt and jeans, but I've suffered through worse. Speaking of which, the offer still stands. We'd really love to have you in the wedding."

"I'm not really a wedding kind of guy. Love and marriage and forever and ever..." He gave a shudder. "Not my thing."

"You don't have to marry anyone. You'll just be standing up with me."

"Maybe next time."

"There won't be a next time." Cody looked so certain that Brent almost believed him.

He might have if not for the all important fact that his brother was a friggin' *vampire*. Translation? Temporary. Things might be picture perfect now, but it wouldn't last. While Miranda herself seemed cool with it, there were others who wouldn't be so accepting. Someone would eventually find out that there were bloodsuckers living in Skull Creek and then all hell would break loose. It always did.

Brent had learned that firsthand and it was a lesson he didn't intend to forget. He'd barely gotten out of Jamison, Texas, without being staked, and all because he'd been stupid enough to fall in love. Or at least he'd thought it was love. It had been early on, right after he'd been turned. He'd been desperate for his life back. For a sense of normalcy. And then he'd met Lila. She'd been pretty and sweet and just like *that* he'd been able to see the two of them settling down and living happily ever after.

A stupid fantasy. That's all it had been. He'd needed to feel like a man again, just a man, and she'd wanted someone to take care of her. The minute she'd seen the truth, she'd turned on him and run back to her family. Her father had told the entire town. They'd come for him then. Captured him. Tortured him.

They'd known he was a bloodsucker with the strength of ten men. But there'd been five times that many. They'd overpowered him, chained him up, beat him. They'd been ready to stake him, too, but he'd managed to work his hand free just in time. He'd made it out, but barely. He wasn't risking his afterlife or his heart ever again.

Love—if there even was such a thing—sucked, no pun intended, and nothing good could come of it.

Not for Brent.

And certainly not for Cody.

His brother might be playing at normal now, but he wasn't. He never would be and eventually the shit would hit the fan and he would have to leave.

"I've got Dillon compiling a list of all the Rose Braddocks in the United States," Brent told him, determined to pull him onto a safer subject. One he could actually do something about. "Once he's done, I'll start checking them out."

"Before the wedding?"

Cody looked so nervous for a split second that Brent couldn't help himself. "I'll be there next Saturday for the ceremony, I just can't promise anything else."

"You can't or you won't?"

"What difference does it make?" He shrugged. "So what's with the blue? I thought most tuxedos were black?"

"Miranda likes blue. She says it brings out the blue in my eyes."

Brent grinned. "You're worse off than I thought, little bro."

"Yeah," Cody admitted, but there was none of the surprise or worry Brent would have expected at such an admission. His brother actually looked happy. "The house is almost done." When Brent turned a questioning look on Cody, he added, "The one I've been building for the past six months? The one I've told you about a dozen times? My wedding gift to Miranda?" Brent shrugged and Cody added, "They just put the floors in yesterday. There are still a few minor things left to do like the phone jacks and the cable hookup, but for the most part it's finished. I spent the day out there yesterday to make sure everything got done."

"With workers in and out?"

"There's a basement that locks from the inside. The workers only have access to the front door." His gaze met Brent's. "If you need a place to crash, I keep a key stashed near the front porch that unlocks the basement. You could camp out until the wedding."

"The motel's just fine."

"I'd really like you to take a look and tell me what you think about the place."

"Does it matter what I think?"

"No," his brother said in all honesty, "but I'd still like you to see it. It's out off old Farm Road 86, about six miles past the turn-off. We could head over after this and I could show you around."

Brent shook his head. "I'm meeting Dillon. So do you have a guest list?" he asked, suddenly eager to ease the flash of disappointment in his brother's gaze. Cody's expression quickly shifted into surprise, and Brent added, "Just because I'm not your best man doesn't mean I can't throw you a bachelor party."

"You don't have to—"

"Just hand it over. A week from tonight. Mark your calendar." He took the paper Cody pulled from his pocket and shoved it into his jeans. Pushing to his feet, he said, "I gotta go."

"I was thinking you might want to stop off after you swing by Dillon's and hang out with me and Miranda. I know she would love it. She wants to get to know you."

"Dillon has a lot leads. It might take a while."

Cody looked ready to argue, but then he shrugged. "Keep me posted."

Brent nodded and walked out of the bridal shop.

Ten minutes later, he pulled into the parking lot of a renovated service station with a neon blue sign that read *Skull Creek Choppers* gleaming in the front glass window. It was the last place he would expect to find a nest of vampires, but then that was the point. The place was ultra small town with its antique gas pumps and old-fashioned *Goo Goo Clusters* sign. Unassuming. Inconspicuous.

Safe.

For now, Brent reminded himself. It wouldn't last. It never lasted.

He rang the buzzer on the high tech security pad sitting next to the door. A split-second later, a lock released and the door opened. He walked into the small room that housed the office portion of the motorcycle manufacture. A tall, muscular man sat in front of a state-of-the-art computer system. He didn't glance up. He didn't have to.

Dillon Cash was a computer guru and the third member of the infamous trio that made up Skull Creek Choppers. He worked with Jake McCall and Garrett Sawyer, both vampires and geniuses when it came to chopper design and construction. Brent had never ridden one of their bikes because he was more of a muscle car kind of guy, but he'd admired their designs more than once.

"So what's up?" he asked Dillon. "Did you find anything specific?"

"Not yet, but I've posted several comments on the different vampire blogs out there detailing Rose and her physical description. It's a long shot, but it worked once before when we were looking for Garrett's maker." He handed over a list of different blog sites. "I'll be keeping an eye on the comments, but you might want to check things out to. That way if anyone posts anything that sounds familiar to you, you can let me know. In the meantime, I did a search for every Rose Braddock in the continental United States."

"And?"

"There are over three hundred of them. I ruled some out based on background, birth certificates, etc., which leaves one hundred and thirty-six possibilities. That is, if she's even using her same name." Dillon handed over a print-out. "I'm doing more detailed searches to narrow it down, but it's going to take time. Speaking of which," he glanced at his watch, "I've got to run. I printed out the various blogs I commented on if you want to monitor them yourself. You might recognize something familiar. Meanwhile, we bide our time and keep looking."

"What's the hurry?"

"It's date night. If I'm late, she'll kill me." He grinned. "Again."

"Damn straight I will." The comment came from the attractive blonde who appeared in the doorway. Brent caught her gaze, but he couldn't read anything behind the twinkle in her eyes.

She came up to Dillon and slid an arm around him. "We need to hurry. The movie starts in five minutes." Her gaze met Brent's. "How's the search going?"

"It's going."

"Keep the faith. If she's out there, Dillon will find her." She smiled up at Dillon. "He found Garrett's maker."

"That's what I've been told. Thanks, man."

"Don't mention it," Dillon said.

"Do you have a girlfriend?" the female vampire asked point-blank.

"Excuse me?"

"Do you have a girlfriend?"

"I don't do girlfriends."

"Ahh," a knowing gleam lit her eyes, "a boyfriend then."

"I don't have a boyfriend either."

She shrugged. "Give it some time. You'll meet Mr. Right soon."

"I'm not gay."

"A player?"

"Something like that."

"Is it?" She leveled an intense stare at him. "Something like that? Because if not and you're a halfway decent guy who's just a little shy, I've got a really great girl I'd like you to meet."

"Meg," Dillon warned, "you promised you wouldn't play Cupid."

"I'm not playing Cupid. It's just that I hired this new girl at the dress shop and she doesn't know very many people in town. I'm guessing Brent here doesn't either and nobody should be alone on a Friday night." Her gaze shifted to Brent. "My friend's name is Daphne. She's really anxious to meet a good guy."

His gut tightened and a frown pulled at his mouth. "I'm not a guy."

"I know what you are."

"Then you'll understand when I say thanks, but no thanks." He nodded at Dillon and then he turned and walked out because the last thing Brent Braddock needed was a fix-up.

He could get his own friggin' date. If he wanted one, which he most certainly did not. He didn't need company, he needed to feed again. Maybe then he could stop thinking about Abby and how badly he'd wanted to press her up against his car and feel her curves up close and personal.

His groin twisted, pressing against his jeans as he walked out of the shop. Hell, he still wanted to, a feeling that intensified when he pulled up at the Skull Creek Inn and saw her car sitting in the parking lot.

His stomach hollowed out and he sat there for a few minutes, staring, wanting.

What the hell was she doing here?

But he already knew. They were smack dab in the middle of small town central. Skull Creek wasn't exactly a tourist mecca which meant the Skull Creek Inn was it when it came to motels. Damn straight she'd be here.

But understanding it didn't make it any easier to swallow. He needed to stop thinking about her and with this new turn of events, he wasn't placing any bets on that possibility. He stiffened as he caught sight of her through the lobby window. His muscles clenched and electricity sizzled up his spine. Anticipation coiled inside him and his gut contracted.

His fangs tingled as he watched her follow Winona down the concrete walkway toward his room. They stopped just one door shy and Winona shoved the key into the lock.

No way. No friggin' way.

Even as the thought struck, Winona pushed open the door and led Abby inside. A switch clicked and yellow light spilled through the slats of the shade that covered the room's one and only window. He caught a glimpse of Abby, her eyes sparkling and her lips slightly parted, before the shade closed. The air conditioning unit groaned and started chugging away, keeping time with the frantic race of adrenalin through his veins.

She'd checked into the room right next to his. Forget pushing her out of his head and avoiding her for the next few weeks. He was sure to run into her

again. That and there was no escaping the fact that
he was a vampire. Meaning, despite sheetrock and
tacky wallpaper, he would be able to hear her. Smell
her. Feel her. Want her.

Like hell.

He keyed the ignition, shoved the car into reverse
and peeled out of the parking lot. And then he headed
for his brother's place.

6

THE FAMILIAR ROAR of an engine echoed in Abby's ears and awareness rippled through her. She glanced at the motel room door and fought down the sudden urge to haul it open and see who was outside.

But she already knew.

The notion struck and she quickly pushed it aside. Just because the engine was loud, didn't mean it belonged to a '67 Camaro. That was her own wishful thinking caused by deprived hormones and a desperate lack of sleep.

She gave herself a mental shake and forced her attention back to the old woman standing in front of her.

"…looks like you got lucky tonight." Winona Adkins wore a blue and orange flower print dress, a pair of sagging knee-high panty-hose and white orthopedic shoes. "This is the only room we have open on account of the rodeo is in town, so we upgraded you. This here's the executive suite."

Abby glanced around the ancient room, from the king-sized bed covered with a faded patchwork quilt, to the scarred hardwood floor and the worn nightstand. It was old, but clean. "*Executive* as in minibar?" She'd left her chili dog behind to race after Brent and her stomach was none too happy.

"A full bathroom. All our rooms have a toilet and sink only, but you got the whole enchilada."

Abby thought of a hot shower and how long it had been since she'd felt such a luxury. "Even better."

"The only thing wrong with it is the air conditioner." She motioned to the window unit that made a slow, churning noise. "It's low on Freon, but Jimmy Joe Mercer can't get out here to fix it 'til next week on account of he's fishing at the coast. In the meantime, you'll have to make do with the ceiling fan until another room opens up."

"It'll be fine." She'd done a seven month tou in Iraq. A little Texas heat certainly didn't scare her.

"Maid service is around noon," Winona went on, "but not after two on account of I never miss Dr. Phil." She set the keycard on the nightstand and motioned to a red plastic bucket. "Ice machine's in the lobby and there's a snack machine right next to it.

We also put in a washer and dryer just down the hall if you want to do any personal laundry. But don't go overstuffing the drum 'cause Merle—he's the only washer repairman in town—is with Jimmy Joe." She nailed Abby with a stare. "And don't go stuffing no unmentionables down the toilet either 'cause they talked Lewis Thalman—he's the local plumber—into going with 'em."

"I promise to be very careful."

"We also offer free muffins every morning." Winona rounded the bed. Wrinkled hands reached for the comforter and folded down the edges. "But you have to get to the lobby before eight if you want the blueberry ones 'cause that's my Eldin's favorite. He's my grandson." She smoothed the blankets and shot a glance at Abby's ringless finger. "He's single, you know. Makes a decent living managing this place for my daughter who moved to Port Aransas with her husband last year. He's got nice eyes, all his own teeth, and his plumbing works like clockwork."

"All the qualities any woman could want in a man."

"Exactly." Winona gave her a sly grin. "I could introduce the two of you when he gets back from Bingo."

"Thanks for the offer, but I'm afraid I already have a boyfriend," she blurted, remembering the lie she'd told Brent Braddock. "I mean, we broke up, but I'm hoping things might still work out."

Instead of giving her a skeptical look, Winona smiled. "Well, what do you know?" She pulled a business card from her pocket and handed it to Abby. "This just might be your lucky day."

Abby stared at the card and a bolt of shock ripped through her. A purple penis, complete with a top hat and eyes, danced across the white vellum. Beneath the image, Winona's name blazed in neon purple letters, followed by the title *Pleasure Consultant*.

O-kay.

"I got an official degree and everything on-line at PleasureConsultants.com," Winona rushed on. "I help women by teaching 'em how to keep the sparks flyin' in their relationships. Host a class right here in the motel lobby every Tuesday night. First one is free, but then you got to pay per lesson like everybody else. This week we're doing *BJ Techniques That Don't End in a Trip to the ER*. It's all about watching the teeth, you know. That, or you can just take 'em out first."

"I really hate to miss that," *not*, "but I'm only in town for a few days."

"That's what they all say." Winona waved a hand. "Don't you worry. I've seen more than one guest add a few days to their trip once they see me in action on the motel's informational channel." At Abby's surprised look, she added, "It's a small town, sugar, not Mars. We got cable, too. 'Course, the reception ain't all that great on account of we're still using rabbit ears on our sets." She motioned toward the 22-inch TV that sat in the corner. "You have to stand near the window and hold a coat hanger if you want to get rid of the snow. But that's just for HBO. The informational channel comes directly from Eldin's computer in the lobby, so the picture is crystal clear."

"You have your own podcast?"

"It's pre-recorded. We ain't figured out how to do a live one just yet. But my Eldin signed up for one of those on-line video editing courses last year. Took bits and pieces of all my classes for the past six months and put them together on one DVD that runs every hour along with check-out instructions, lobby hours and a listing of local attractions. There's a bake sale over at the Lion's Club tomorrow. Got the best German Chocolate cake around. I'm thinking I'll pick up a few for Tuesday night's class."

Sex *and* cake. It didn't get much better than that.

Winona waddled over to a nearby closet and pulled a few extra blankets from the top shelf. She set them on a small chair before flashing Abby a narrowed gaze. "But just 'cause I believe couples should have plenty of sex, doesn't mean I ain't a decent, God-fearing woman. This here's a respectable establishment." She wagged an arthritic finger. "We don't allow no parties or loud music or carrying on. And we surely don't allow no swearing or cussing." She turned toward the door. "Unless you're telling off old Zeke Mitchell from the gas station next door," she paused, hand on the knob. "Why, he sneaks over here every morning to snag our newspaper while my Eldin is picking up muffins at the bakery. Talk about a cheap SOB." The click of the latch punctuated the statement. Hinges creaked. Shoes squeaked. And Winona was gone.

Abby blinked and stared at the piece of vellum in her hand. Thanks to the military, she'd been all over the world. She'd seen it all—power hungry czars, crazed dictators, brutal extremists.

But she could honestly say she'd never, ever seen a seventy-something-year-old pleasure consultant with a dancing penis business card.

Tonight was definitely a first.

In more ways than one.

The thought struck and Brent's image walked into her head. Her stomach hollowed out and she remembered the intense desire she'd felt when she'd stared into his eyes. The overwhelming urge to forget everything—her duty, her plan, her objective—and act on it.

She'd wanted to.

She still did.

Electricity hummed over her skin and her nerves buzzed. She felt antsy. Wired. This close to the edge. As if something was about to happen and she was counting down the seconds.

She shook aside the strange sensation and headed for the bathroom. A shower and a good night's sleep would fix everything. Her muscles would relax. The exhaustion would take over. And then Brent Braddock would be history.

That's what she told herself, but the minute the warm water hit her skin, her senses fired fully to life. The hot rivulets streamed over her flesh and she started to tingle in all the right places. Or rather, the wrong places given her current situation and the fact that she couldn't afford to lose her focus. Her thighs clenched. Her nipples tightened.

Don't think. Just go through the motions and get the job done.

She reached for the soap. The ripe strawberry scent spiraled through her nostrils and the pink lather tickled the insides of her fingers. She slid the soap back into the tray and ran her soapy hands up and down her arms. Over her shoulders. Between her breasts. Down the planes of her stomach and lower. Until she reached the fleshy mound between her legs.

Her hands trembled and she twisted the tap. Cold water blasted over her, killing the sensations. There. That was better. Bearable.

She stood under the icy spray for several minutes, until her heartbeat slowed and her determination returned full force. She could do this. She could push him out of her mind and concentrate on her mission. She could.

Turning off the water, she reached for a towel and padded into the bedroom. She pulled on a tank top and panties, killed the lights and climbed between the sheets. She closed her eyes and tuned in to the slow groan of the air conditioner. It whined and sputtered, spitting out lukewarm air that soon had her kicking off the covers.

Laying there, she stared at the ceiling fan and tried to ignore the tickle of perspiration that slid down her temples, the undersides of her breasts. A fine sheen soon covered her skin and her breaths grew frequent and more shallow until she just couldn't seem to get enough air.

Crazy.

She'd been stranded in the middle of a desert in the high heat of day before and never felt this feverish. But tonight was different. An edge hung in the air. Expectancy twisted her stomach tight. The stifling atmosphere closed in, pressing down and suffocating her.

She pushed to her feet, hauled on a pair of shorts and grabbed the ice bucket. She'd done hot before, but this was ridiculous.

Then again, the temperature had nothing to do with the failing air conditioner and everything to do with the Camaro parked in front of the motel.

She came up short in the open doorway and stared at the familiar black muscle car sitting next to her rental. She hadn't heard him pull in because she'd probably been fighting her hormones in the shower, but it didn't change the fact that he was here. And that on a deeper level, she'd been completely aware of his presence.

That's why she'd been so restless.

So needy.

So hot.

She drew in as much oxygen as she could gather, steeled herself and hooked a left down the walkway toward the front office. A few minutes later, she arrived back in her room with a bucket full of ice. She fought the split-second urge to knock on his door before rushing inside her own and slamming and locking it behind her. Grabbing a plastic cup, she made herself a glass of ice water and chugged every last drop. She twisted the temperature knob on the air unit down as far as it would go, opened up the few windows that ran on the back wall and stretched out on top of the sheets. Closing her eyes, she concentrated on the coolness that lingered in her mouth and pictured herself on a snowy mountaintop in Afghanistan. Freezing and miserable and sweaty.

Wait a second.

There'd been no sweating on that mountaintop. No buzzing nerves. No tingling nipples. She'd been this close to freezing to death and her only thought had been survival.

Not him and the way his lips tugged slightly more at the right corner of his mouth when he smiled or the way his eyes glittered so brightly whenever they snagged on her mouth.

Survival, she reminded herself. Think chattering teeth and numb fingers and tingling toes—

Bam!

The slam of a door shattered her thoughts. Her breath caught and every nerve jumped to awareness. Her ears tuned to the steady thud of footsteps. The creak of a mattress. A radio flicked on and Tim McGraw started singing about bad boys and good men and, well, the *last* thing she needed to think about was either one.

Brent Braddock was back and he was right next door.

7

JUST BREATHE. She forced her eyes shut and did a deep breathing exercise to soothe her jumpiness. She'd learned the technique to deal with the extreme pressure of being in the field and it had always worked every time.

Until now.

With the song playing and the occasional *thud* and *creak* from next door, she couldn't seem to slow her lungs enough to relax. Not when she kept picturing him stretched out naked on the bed. His tanned body dark and sensual against the paleness of the sheets. His muscles tight and bulging with sexual tension. His eyes blazing with—

She sat up and killed the image. With trembling hands, she reached for the remote and hit the ON button. Winona's voice crackled over the speaker, drowning out the sounds drifting from next door. She cranked up the volume as loud as it could go.

"…when a marriage gets a little stale, it's time for fantasy role play to spice things up. There ain't a woman alive who doesn't go all weak in the knees when she thinks about being captured by a pirate or forced into submission by a high falutin' sheik. It's the same for a man. While he would never nail a real milkmaid, especially since the only one around here has a mustache and goes by the name of Hank, he still entertains the fantasy every now and then. Not about Hank, but about his woman. He'd like to see her in a short skirt and little suspenders. That, or he'd like to see her as a sexy nurse or a gypsy or one of them there hot-to-trot flight attendants. So let's get busy, ladies. Dress up, turn him on and help him land that plane right smack dab down the center of that runway…"

Abby had a quick visual of herself clad in a flight attendant's outfit sitting astride a very sexy Captain Brent and her thighs clenched. The temperature seemed to kick up a few blazing degrees and she reached for the glass of ice sitting on the nightstand.

She grabbed an ice cube and touched it to her lips. Icy liquid drizzled down the corner of her mouth, winding a path down her neck. She slid the cube down over her chin, to the pounding pulse beat. The hard chunk felt cool and soothing. *Cool*, as in the opposite of hot. If she could just focus on the sensation, she might be able to forget the fire burning her up from the inside out.

Moving the ice even lower, she slid it over her collarbone, down between her breasts. The frigid touch grazed the tip of one nipple and she stiffened. Electricity zipped up her spine and a gasp caught on her lips. Her skin grew tighter. Itchier. Hotter.

This was definitely not helping.

No, there was only one thing that would help ease her frustrated hormones—sating said hormones. Not that she was about to knock on Brent's door and ask for a quickie. Hardly. While her body might crave him, the reality was that she could handle this all by herself. She'd done it before and it made the morning after a lot less complicated.

One orgasm coming right up!

She grabbed another piece of ice and touched it to the quivering bud of her clit. Hunger spurted through her and her nerves hummed. The air seemed to shimmer and her heart started to pound. She slid the hard coolness along the length of her hot slit. The ice melted against her blazing flesh, drip-dropping between her fingers and gliding down her palm as she moved back and forth. The coldness quickly disappeared, until only her fingertips rasped the swollen flesh.

She didn't meant to fantasize about him, but she couldn't help herself. Through a haze of pleasure she saw him standing there wearing nothing but a pair of jeans and a hungry expression.

Watching.

Waiting.

The notion sent a rush of excitement through her and she slid a finger inside her drenched heat. Her body clenched and she moved her hips, riding the sensation, drawing it deeper until her breath quickened and a cry worked its way up her throat. The room seemed to explode in a burst of color as she arched, holding on to the feeling for a long, brilliant moment.

"Beautiful."

The deep, familiar voice slid into her ears and jerked her back to reality. Her eyes snapped open, and that's when she realized that it wasn't just her erotic imagination at work.

Brent Braddock stood, live and in color, at the foot of her bed.

She blinked, but he didn't disappear. Shock ripped through her and she bolted to a sitting position. Scrambling for the sheet, she stuffed it under each arm. "What are you doing here?" she blurted, her heart pounding out of her chest.

"Enjoying the view." The deep, seductive voice whispered through her head so clear and distinct that she could have sworn he spoke the words.

He didn't. The only movement of his mouth was the faintest crook of a grin. Slow. Subtle. Sexy.

Her heart skipped its next beat.

"I heard a scream," he finally murmured. "I thought you might need help."

"I stubbed my toe." It wasn't the most original lie, but it was the best she could do with him standing so close and staring so intently. "It hurt, so I yelped."

His brows drew together. "It didn't sound like a yelp. It sounded like a full-fledged—"

"How did you get in here?" she cut in, eager to distract herself from the heat creeping up her spine. "I locked the door."

"You must have made a mistake." He shrugged. "It opened right up."

Her mind did a quick rewind. She felt the metal against her fingers. Heard the click of the deadbolt. "I don't make those kinds of mistakes."

"There's a first for everything." He cocked an eyebrow. "How else would I be here?"

He had a point. He couldn't very well have slipped through the keyhole. He was six foot plus of solid, hunky muscle. Half-naked and devastatingly handsome.

Half-naked and devastatingly sexy.

He wore only a pair of faded jeans. Muscle sculpted his chest and arms. Slave band tattoos, the pattern dark and intricate, circled each bicep. Hair sprinkled his chest from nipple to nipple before funneling into a silky swirl that followed a decadent path that bisected a very impressive six pack before disappearing beneath the waistband of his jeans. A frayed rip in the denim gave her a sneak peak of one muscular thigh dusted with hair.

She had the sudden image of that thigh flush against hers, his body pressing her down into the mattress, his lips eating at hers, and her mouth went dry.

"Let me take a look at your toe." His deep voice pushed into her head and snatched her back to reality and the all important fact that she was naked beneath the sheet and he was still standing there. His pale green eyes darkened to an impenetrable jade and her stomach hollowed out. "To see how badly you're hurt."

She pulled her knees up to her chest beneath the sheet and tucked the cotton more securely under each arm. "It's fine. Really. No permanent damage." She summoned a smile and tried to ignore the urge to jump up and pull him down onto the bed with her. "Thanks for checking on me."

"Anytime."

The word held a wealth of meaning and lingered in her head long after the door closed behind him.

As if he really and truly wanted her as badly as she wanted him.

He didn't.

She knew that.

She'd always known that when it came to men.

She was a plain cookie in a bakery full of chunky decadence. And no man in his right mind would sink his teeth into the ho-hum sugar variety when he could have quarter-size pieces of melt-in-your-mouth chocolate or M & Ms or peanut butter. It just didn't happen that way. Men didn't lust after her. Or flirt. Or send suggestive signals.

Especially men like Brent Braddock. He was way out of her league with his smoking body and his raw sensuality. No way was she reading his signals correctly.

At the same time, that's what she did. She read people for a living and assessed every situation. It was her job and she was good at it. Even more, she didn't make careless mistakes.

He wanted her. He really and truly *wanted* her.

And she wanted him.

A truth that had her powering on the TV again, desperate for a distraction.

"It's all about dressing for success, Ladies." Winona stared back at her from the television screen.

It was the last thing she needed to watch, but she found herself tuning in anyway for lack of anything better.

At least that's what she told herself.

"If you want your man to notice you, you have to go the extra mile," Winona went on. "And if you want him to *really* notice you, you need to do it with the minimum amount of clothing because men like to see skin. Lots and lots of skin. And a slutty pair of high heels don't hurt none either. We've got several shops right here in Skull Creek where you can buy a decent pair of tramp shoes…"

Winona droned on about the need for high heels and how they made the legs look longer and the boobs look bigger. It was nothing Abby hadn't heard before in the girls' locker room back in high school. Of course, she'd never had such an interesting visual to go with the gossip (namely Winona parading around in a pair of silver sandals with blinking red lights on the toes). Yes, she'd heard it over and over, but she'd never tried it.

Not then and certainly not now. She was fine with

her life. Fulfilled. She didn't need sexy clothes. Or sexy men. Or another orgasm.

She needed to find Rayne. End of story.

That's why she'd come here in the first place. To find her man.

Her man. Not just any man. And certainly not one as hot and sexy as Brent Braddock. She didn't need that kind of distraction right now.

Even if she suddenly wanted one.

Letting loose a deep sigh, she kicked off the covers, forced her eyes shut and settled in for the longest, most restless night of her life.

8

IT WAS THE EARLY hours of the morning and Brent was doing his damnedest to shut out the sounds coming from the next room and forget the woman stretched out on the bed. He wasn't thinking about her. He was sleeping. Right here. Right now.

He clamped his eyes shut and punched at his pillow. *Sleep.* The silent command echoed in his head, quickly drowned out by a soft sigh and the rustle of sheets.

He turned onto his opposite side, punched at the pillow and tried again.

Ka-thunk, ka-thunk, ka-thunk…

The steady beat slid into his ears, a soft, subtle sound that kept time with his own heartbeat.

Shit.

He turned onto his back and stared at the ceiling.

Instead of seeing the white plaster, he saw Abby. Her long, loose hair draped over the pillow. Her knees parted. Her skin covered with a fine sheen of sweat. Her lips parted on a gasp. Her hands working at the ice.

His groin clenched and he damned himself a thousand times for going over there in the first place.

He'd tried to resist. He'd turned on the radio to drown out the noise, taken a cold shower, given himself a great big mental kick in the ass and climbed into bed determined to sleep.

But then he'd heard her sharp intake of breath and the bubble of a gasp as she'd touched the ice to her skin, and he'd stopped thinking altogether. The rule about not being able to enter a dwelling unless invited didn't apply to motels or other public establishments where people came and went and so, in a flash, he'd been at the foot of her bed. Watching. Wanting.

Holy shit.

He knew better. He'd always known better and so he kept his distance whenever he settled in any one place. No getting to know anyone. No making friends.

It wasn't a reality he liked, but it was the way things were and he was used to it.

Hell, he *liked* it.

He'd learned the hard way with Lila. They'd had plans that had all gone to hell in a handbasket because of what he'd become. She'd turned on him and he'd had to run for his life.

He'd learned at that moment that the less he knew, the less he cared, the easier it was to leave.

And leaving was inevitable.

As soon as the thought struck, he thought of Cody and Miranda and the new house his brother had just built.

A friggin' idiot. That's what Cody was, chasing some ridiculous happily ever after. Brent knew firsthand that it wouldn't work. He'd almost been killed that night Lila had turned on him. While the scars had faded, the memory of each lash was as vivid as if it had happened yesterday. Sure vampires healed rapidly, but they still felt pain. More intensely than most because their senses were so heightened.

Settling down was a bad idea. Getting attached to one woman was even worse. And building a friggin' house? Talk about jumping off the deep end.

He told himself that as he listened to the soft sounds of Abby's breathing. Winona's voice played in the background, but it was Abby he heard. The slide of skin across the sheets. The soft in and out of each breath. The occasional gasp when Winona said something particularly shocking.

The noises vibrated in the air, brushed across his skin and stirred his already aroused body until his fangs tingled and his dick throbbed and he reached his limit. Pushing to his feet, he pulled on a T-shirt, hauled on his boots and grabbed his keys.

He meant to drive around and clear his head. That was it. Just some blessed distance to regain his perspective. But then he saw the turn off for Farm Road 86 and he couldn't help himself. He hung a left and drove a few miles until he saw an old cattle guard on his right. He bounced over the metal and headed down the dirt road. Pasture stretched endlessly to his left and his right and he punched the gas harder. Gravel and dirt flew in his rearview mirror and the wind rushed through the open windows.

By the time he spotted the two-story ranch house, he'd worked off enough tension that he could actually think. Pulling up in front, he killed the engine and climbed out.

A construction dumpster sat off to the right and a pile of dirt to the left. The driveway had yet to be poured, but otherwise the house was just about finished. The outside was a combination of white hill country rock and tan stucco. A massive porch stretched the full length of the first floor. It was the kind of house made for lots of kids and big Christmases and Sunday barbecues.

Not that Cody could have any of that. His little brother was pretending. Setting himself up for heartache.

Brent walked the perimeter of the massive house before he wound up back in front. True to Cody's word, he'd left a key stashed under a rock to the right of the porch. Sliding the metal into the lock, Brent turned the doorknob and walked into the large entryway. He went from room to room, his boots echoing on the hardwood floor and bouncing off the walls.

With every modern convenience, vaulted ceilings and granite countertops, it was nothing like the old ranch house where they'd grown up so long ago.

At the same time, it felt exactly the same. Warmth radiated from the vanilla colored walls and embraced him, and as he walked from room to room, he didn't feel so cold.

Cody had been right.

It was nice.

It was home.

The minute the thought struck, he kicked it right back out. He'd lost his home a long time ago. His family. Even though his brothers were still around, things were different. They were different. The relationship, the closeness, the family bond they'd had,

had all been shattered. They were all on their own now. Alone.

Just the way he liked it.

He flipped off the lights and darkness smothered the strange sense of melancholy that had slipped through him. His vision sharpened and focused and he walked down the main hallway, through the kitchen until he found the door leading to the basement.

A few seconds later, he collapsed on the cot that had been set up underground for the times when Cody must have pulled an all-nighter to finish the house in time. The quiet settled around him as he closed his eyes and he welcomed a wave of relief.

Better. Much better.

He didn't have to hear her every sigh or smell the sweet scent of her shampoo or imagine what she looked like stretched out on the bed, or how easy it would be to barge into her room and take what he so desperately wanted.

He'd come close. Dangerously close.

Never again.

From this moment on, he was thinking with his head, not his cock, and keeping his distance the way he always did.

He could get by on blood alone. He didn't *need* to have sex with Abby. The damned trouble of it all was that it was the one thing he *wanted*. The only thing.

And he knew deep down that his lust would eventually win out. And all hell would break loose when it did.

THE LAST THING Abby needed was a pair of high heels.

She told herself that the next morning as she stood outside of *The Sweet Stuff*. It was one of the clothing stores Winona had mentioned in her infomercial about dressing for sexcess. Not that Abby needed sexcess.

The only thing she really needed was to buy a decent outfit that made her look like the jilted girlfriend rather than—to quote Dolly—a Unibomber. With combat boots and dog tags, no one would buy that she could even attract a man, much less that she'd had a bonafide relationship with one. Particularly Rayne Montana. He'd been definite man candy.

To other women, of course. She'd always been so focused on work that she hadn't spared him much attention. There'd been no chemistry. No instant *wow* like she felt with Brent.

Her memory stirred and she saw him standing at the foot of the bed. Definite wow.

Not that it mattered. She was on a mission and priority number one was finding Rayne.

He was hot which meant he would have settled down with an equally hot woman. Hence the outfit change.

Still, she wasn't buying a pair of high heels or strappy sandals or stiletto boots with studs. A pair of flip flops or ballet flats would work just fine.

There was no reason to go overboard even if she did sort of like the silver lace up high heel sandals in the front window. If she'd been in the market for slut shoes, they would have made the top of her list. But slutty and feminine were two different things. One attracted a man and the other screamed *trust me, I'm a poor jilted female.*

Since she was, in fact, playing the jilted female, she wasn't trying to attract anyone. She didn't have time to play dress up for some man, even if she'd liked the way a certain man had looked at her last night when he'd stood at the foot of her bed.

As if he'd wanted to lay her down and love her within an inch of her life.

The heat of the moment.

That's what she'd decided.

Any man would have been turned on by a nearly naked female masturbating with ice. It wasn't because Brent actually liked her.

It didn't matter. That's what she'd realized last night. It had felt good to feel desired. To feel beautiful. She'd felt both for those few moments when he'd looked at her. She'd felt like a woman and she'd liked it. A lot.

Not enough to think that Hockey Guy was a fluke. She knew she wasn't cut out to prance around in high heels and dresses in the real world. It wasn't who she really was. It never would be.

But for a little while?

Her gaze went to the silver sandals and the red dress on display just above it. Both definitely screamed *I have a vagina and I know how to use it.* She couldn't help but wonder how Brent would look at her if she wore something like that. The same way he'd looked at her last night? Would he be turned on enough to actually touch her this time? Kiss her?

She entertained the possibility all of five seconds before drop-kicking it back out. She had work to do. She had two weeks to find Rayne or her butt was going in the frying pan. Her future was at stake, and she'd always put her career over her own needs.

Her mind made up, she drew a deep breath and pushed open the door.

9

AN HOUR LATER, Abby walked out of the clothing shop wearing a brand new outfit with two extra bags on her arms. Plenty to tide her over for the next few days while she tracked down Rayne. A pair of silver ballet flats clung to her feet and a pink sundress the sales clerk had insisted complimented her complexion swirled around her knees.

While she'd never been much for pink, she had to admit that it did give her cheeks some color. And the cut wasn't so bad either. The bodice hugged her chest and actually made her look a cup size larger. The skirt itself flowed over her hips, disguising their fullness and making her look as if she had a waist. She had the fleeting thought that she'd been missing out all these years in her combat boots and baggy fatigues.

But then a strap crept down her shoulder, reminding her that her body just wasn't made for all this girl stuff. She hiked the cotton back up, tightened her grip on her bags and headed for the rental car that sat parked at a nearby curb.

It was a typical Saturday morning on Main Street and people walked to and fro. Two old men sat outside of the diner working on a crossword puzzle. A girl scout stood on the corner selling cookies. Tossing her bags into the trunk, she locked up the car and headed for the pharmacy that stood next to the clothing shop. It was time to get to work.

Pushing through the glass double doors, she scoped out the interior. An old-fashioned soda fountain sat off to the right. Red stools lined the counter that spanned the length of the wall. Straight ahead, a tall man with a shiny bald head and a white lab coat worked behind a clear plastic partition. A fifty-something brunette with a ten-gallon hairdo worked the small counter in front of him. She wore a similar white lab coat, a pair of rhinestone-studded cat's eye glasses and a pen tucked behind one ear.

Abby walked up as she keyed in a prescription for the customer in front of her.

"I'm tellin' you, Charmaine, we don't sell nothin' like that. This here's a pharmacy. We got your usual sundries, but you'll need to go on-line to one of them sex shops if you want a vibrator."

"I don't want a vibrator. I'm interested in a hand-held massager." The customer rubbed at her neck. "For stiff muscles. The doc says it'll help even more than the pain medicine. You sure you don't have one stashed in the back?"

The clerk shook her head. "We ain't had none since Maybelle Dupree gave herself a bad burn last year, if you know what I mean. Elmer," she pointed to the white lab coat-clad man who stood in the back measuring out a bottle of pills, "refused to stock any-more of 'em. Says he ain't setting himself up for a lawsuit because half the women in this town are un-dersexed and don't know how to read the operating instructions. It said plain as day right there on the label—For External Use Only. Why, she had to go to the emergency room and everything."

"I heard about that," Charmaine said. "Heard tell it took three doctors and a nurse to dislodge the thing."

"It was four," the clerk corrected, "and I heard there's still a piece missing."

"No wonder she looked so happy when I saw her dancing at the VFW hall last week."

"Ain't that the truth." The clerk nodded, hand-ing over the prescription and the woman's change. "I heard Doo or Dye is offering massages now. Got one of the hair stylists doin' it in between the perms and the colors. You ought to check that out." The clerk turned her attention to Abby. "Name?"

"Abby. Abby Trenton."

"Trenton with a T," the woman murmured as she turned toward the massive drawers that lined the wall. "I'm afraid it's not here. When did you drop it off, hon?"

"I didn't. I'm not here for a prescription." She pasted on her most hopeful expression. "I was hoping I could ask you a few questions."

"Elmer," the woman called over her shoulder. "Better get that space cleaned up back there. The Feds are here again."

"I'm not a government official."

One perfectly penciled eyebrow shot up. "Not even the IRS?"

"No."

"Jimmy Jo's Detective Agency? Landsakes, I told Elmer not to go off meeting that redhead from the diner for lunch. Pauline's on to you," she called over her shoulder to the man behind the glass partition. "I knew it was only a matter of time."

"We're just friends," Elmer called out as he filled a plastic container with tiny white pills. "She likes to play dominoes."

"I'm not a detective," Abby told the clerk. "I'm a receptionist. From out of town. I'm here looking for an ex-boyfriend of mine. His name is Rayne Montana."

The woman's gaze went wide with excitement. "You're Rayne's girlfriend?"

"Do you know him?"

"Everybody knows him, honey. He grew up around here. Lived his whole life just up the road."

"What about recently?"

"Sure enough. He's been living out at his grandma's place just over the railroad tracks. At least, he was. I ain't seen him around for the past few weeks. Not since he left on his honeymoon."

Abby had anticipated a lot of scenarios, but this hadn't been one of them. "He's married? Are you sure?"

"Didn't watch 'em tie the knot myself—they kept it small with friends and family only—but Milly Haskins heard about it from Darlene Chapin who heard from Ethel McIntosh who heard from her daughter, who's a waitress at the bar where Lucy—that's his wife—works. Said it was a nice little ceremony—rose petals down the aisle, huge flower sprays on every row, violin music and everything."

"*Married*?" She tried to digest the turn of events. He'd gone AWOL and endangered everyone in their unit to come home and get *married*? He'd never even had a girlfriend to Abby's knowledge. Sure, he'd mentioned an old high school flame once or twice, but there'd been no letters from home. No trips back for the holidays. He'd always spent any time on leave volunteering for extra assignments. Keeping busy. Filling the void because he'd had no family to return to. No home.

Abby knew the feeling because she'd done the same. With her father gone, she'd had no one to share the holidays with. Even before, they'd never celebrated much. No big turkey. No massive tree. No presents.

Her father had believed in discipline and structure and self-sacrifice. There'd been no rushing down the stairs on Christmas morning. No rummaging through the stockings. No giggling and laughing over turkey.

Not that she'd wanted those things. Okay, maybe she had once or twice, but the bottom line is that she'd been fine without them. She was fine now. And Rayne had been, as well. Or so she'd thought.

"You're sure we're talking about the same Rayne Montana?"

"Trust me. We ain't got an overabundance of 'em around here. He's spoken for, sugar. So if I was you, I'd head back home and forget all about him."

"I can't do that."

The clerk arched an eyebrow and her eyes danced with excitement. "You ain't knocked up are you?"

"Of course not."

The excitement disappeared. "Then go home, get even and forget all about him. That's what I did with Harley. He's my ex. Broke up with me on the one year anniversary of our first date. Instead of showing up at my house with an engagement ring, he showed up with Ellen Carlysle. Told me they were running away together to Del Rio and that he wanted his pearl handle hunting knife back on account of they were going hog hunting together. I slammed the door in his face, put the knife up on eBay and then gave specific measurements of his privates on my Facebook page. Length *and* diameter. Then I headed down to the VFW Hall and found myself a new man, and that's all she wrote." She wiggled her ring finger. "Been married for over six months now." She leveled a stare at Abby. "Forget about him, sugar."

"You don't happen to know where he went, do you?"

"Bermuda, I think. Or maybe it was Bali. Either way, there's no sense running after him. He'll be home by next Saturday. His wife starts summer classes at Travis County Community College the following Monday. She's studying to be an interior designer. Good looking little thing." When she realized what she'd said, she added, "Not as good looking as you, hon. You're much prettier." She swept a gaze over Abby. "I like the pink."

A rush of warmth swept through Abby. A crazy reaction considering she felt about as comfortable as a stuffed sausage. But she went a little warm inside nonetheless and for a split-second, she forgot all about Rayne and her desperation to find him. She thought about Brent and the fire in his eyes and she found herself wondering what he would think about the pink.

Not that it mattered. He wouldn't even see her in it for that matter, since she fully intended to stay as far away from him as possible while she was in Skull Creek. She didn't need the distraction. She needed to concentrate on Rayne.

He'd left the unit for a woman.

As simple as the truth was, it only made the situation that much more complicated. It just didn't add up. It would have been easy for him to leave the military with an honorable discharge rather than risk his reputation by running off. He could have left after his last tour to settle down and start a family rather than re-enlisting, which he'd done three times.

He didn't have to risk a court marshal.

But he'd done just that. He'd gone AWOL and

jeopardized his mission, not to mention his unit. Just like that.

Because of a woman?

The question dogged her as she headed down to the corner diner. It didn't make any sense. A dedicated soldier would never do such a thing and Rayne had been one of the most dedicated. There had to be more to it.

Not that it mattered.

She was here to find him, haul him back and clear her reputation. Not uncover his motives. The MPs could take care of the hows and whys.

She was here to bring him back, period.

Which was exactly what she fully intended to do once he came back. And he would come back. He had a wife now. A family. A home.

A pang of envy rushed through her before she managed to remind herself that she'd never been cut out for the home and hearth thing. She didn't cook. She didn't clean. She didn't stay in any one place for more than a few months. Her job didn't permit it, and her job was everything.

"You're military," her dad had always told her. *"It's in your blood. It's who you are. No sense denying fate."*

He'd been right. The one time she'd tried to change her life, to put on makeup and dress up and be a normal sixteen-year-old girl, Hockey Hunk had laughed in her face.

Abby ignored the strange sense of regret that rushed through her and pushed through the doorway of the diner. She spent the next hour eating chicken fried steak and verifying the clerk's story. Rayne Montana had, according to Doris the waitress and Monty the cook and Ellen and Irma from the Ladies Auxiliary, gotten married in a small, private ceremony two weeks ago to a woman named Lucy Rivers. They'd left on a vacation to the Bahamas/ Bermuda/Bala/fill-in-your-favorite-vacation-spot-that-started-with-a-B. While no one knew exactly where they'd gone, everyone said the same thing— they would be back in time for Lucy to start classes the following week.

It was Saturday and Rayne was expected to return home a week from today, which meant the only thing for Abby to do was bide her time and wait.

While she was relieved that she'd found him, she couldn't shake the restlessness that settled in the pit of her stomach and followed her around for the rest of the day as she scoped out Rayne's old house and visited the bar where Lucy Rivers worked.

A crazy feeling because she'd done more than her share of surveillance over the years. She'd killed endless hours waiting for the right moment to strike.

She'd spent one hundred and sixty-three days down in Guatemala watching the entrance to a cantina, day in and day out, and she hadn't felt nearly the anxiety she felt when she finally made her way back to the motel.

She pulled up next to Brent's Camaro and awareness skittered up and down her spine.

Her knuckles brushed the smooth black finish as she angled between the cars and headed for her motel room. Her hands trembled as she slid her key into the lock and opened her door. Her ears tuned, listening for any sounds, but the only thing she heard was the hum of the air conditioner and the click of her own doorknob.

She tossed her keys aside, flipped on the TV and watched as Winona waltzed around a brass stripper pole and demonstrated proper hand technique when doing a spin. The sight was frightening (we're talking a seventy-something-year-old woman), yet oddly fascinating at the same time. Abby had never actually seen a stripper pole, nor did she know what to do with one. Five minutes with Winona and she felt as if she could grab hold and work it out. She envisioned Brent parked in a chair, watching intently as she strolled back and forth in front of him wearing a racy outfit and sky-high heels. She dropped pieces here and there, teasing him, tempting him.

It was the craziest fantasy because Abby didn't do either when it came to men. But she wanted to.

The realization hit her as she heard the shower turn on next door. The pipes grumbled and the water rushed and she knew that Brent was about to climb in.

Her hands trembled and her nipples pressed tightly against the bodice of the sundress. But she didn't just crave an orgasm. She craved the warmth that had rushed through her last night when she'd become aware that he was standing there, looking at her, wanting her.

The surge of feminine power.

The certainty deep inside that she was every bit the woman she tried so hard to hide.

Just a woman.

Soft and feminine and sexy and vulnerable.

That's how she felt when he looked at her. And while she couldn't afford to feel that way in her daily life—her survival in the field relied on the respect of her men and the power of her authority—she had to admit that it was kind of nice.

For now.

She felt like a beautiful, desirable woman when Brent looked at her and that's what she found herself wanting to feel again. Not just the sweet rush of warmth when she came, but the certainty that he wanted her and only her at that moment.

She had no illusions that he felt more. He didn't really know her. He thought she was the poor, jilted girlfriend, not some ball buster with the military. Should he learn the truth, she had no doubt that he would turn and walk away just like every other man in her past.

Men were intimidated by her. They always had been and they always would be.

But not Brent.

Not yet.

While she wasn't fool enough to think the feeling would last—once he realized the truth about her, he would run the other way like every other man in her past—there suddenly seemed nothing wrong with playing dress up and indulging her feminine side in the meantime.

She reached for one of the shopping bags and pulled out the silver strappy heels and the tight red dress she'd bought on a whim. Her memory stirred and she saw herself standing on the doorstep watching Hockey Hunk leave with the head cheerleader. It had been the most humiliating moment of her life.

Because she'd put her heart on her sleeve.

She hadn't just liked Hockey Hunk. She'd loved him. After months of sitting across from him during tutoring sessions, rooting for him at every game, sharing her lunch on those days when he forgot his, she'd been head over heels for him.

This was different.

This was sex.

And so she didn't have to worry about making a fool of herself. She would be the one walking away this time.

A thrill rushed through her as she ran her hands over the stretchy fabric. It was nothing like anything she would ever wear in real life.

Which was the point entirely.

To abandon her tomboy image and be the woman she'd never allowed herself to be. She was through wondering what it felt like to dress up and tempt a man.

She was going to experience it firsthand.

Starting now.

10

THIS WAS *NOT* GOOD.

The thought struck even before Abby knocked on Brent's door. He knew it the moment she made up her mind to stop resisting and give in to the lust that burned inside of her. It was a knowledge that had nothing to do with his heightened vampire senses and everything to do with the awareness that sizzled in the air around him. The expectancy that settled in his gut. As if something monumental was about to happen and it was just a matter of time.

The feeling dogged him while he finished up his shower. Then a knock sounded on his door, confirming his worst suspicions. His heart skipped a beat as he stepped out of the shower. His hand trembled as he reached for a towel. Excitement zipped up and down his spine and he stiffened.

The last thing he wanted was to see Abby on his doorstep. He needed distance. Safety.

He wiped at the water dripping from his face and knotted the towel at his waist. Another knock sounded and his muscles clenched.

He wasn't going to answer. That's what he told himself. He would pretend to be asleep and slip out once she'd given up.

But then she knocked again and he caught a deep whiff of her sweet shampoo. He reached for the knob.

"Yeah?" He hauled open the door and got the surprise of his afterlife.

She looked nothing like the Plain Jane woman who'd followed him from the Dairy Freeze and everything like the woman he'd glimpsed last night in her bedroom. Sexy. Seductive. Irresistible.

Her dress was short and tight, cut down to there and up to here. Red spandex hugged her voluptuous curves and left little to the imagination. And where there wasn't shiny red fabric, there was skin. Lots and lots of soft, supple, tempting flesh that made his mouth water and his pulse race.

He didn't mean to stare. He meant to play it cool, to close the door and ignore her, but he couldn't help himself.

His gaze shifted up before sweeping back down

and pausing several places in between. The smooth column of her throat. The frantic beat of her pulse. The bare curve of her shoulder. The deep swell of her luscious breasts. The press of her ripe nipples against the thin material that barely passed for a dress. The flare of her hips. The long, bare legs that seemed to go on and on.

"I hope I didn't wake you up," she murmured, only the faintest tremble in her voice giving away that she might be the slightest bit nervous.

"I was in the shower."

"I see that."

And so could he. For a split-second, her guard faltered and he read the thoughts that raced inside her pretty little head. Her gaze drew him in and suddenly he was right there, seeing through her eyes, feeling what she felt, wanting what she wanted.

He'd been partially hidden behind the door when he'd first answered her knock, but he was completely visible now. Visible and nearly naked, with only a towel slung low on his lean hips and water beading on his dark skin.

Nearly naked and oh so close.

She could feel the heat coming off him, smell the enticing aroma of clean soap and virile male. She took a deep breath as her eyes drank in the sight of him. The white cotton wrapped around his lean waist was in stark contrast to his tanned muscle. Broad shoulders framed a hard, sinewy chest sprinkled with dark hair that tapered to a slim line and disappeared beneath the towel's edge. The same hair covered the length of his powerful thighs and calves. He was every bit as hot as she remembered and she gave herself a great big mental kick in the ass for not acting on her feelings sooner.

She wanted him.

Her body clenched and wetness rushed between her legs. She should have reached for him last night, pulled him down, invited him in. She'd held back. She was still holding back, but not because she was afraid. She wanted to fulfill her deepest fantasies. To tempt him with her body and lure him with her smile. She wanted him so hot that he couldn't keep his hands off her. She wanted him to throw her on the bed and strip her bare and lick her from head to toe—

"What do you want?" he blurted, killing the vivid image.

His groin tightened and he stepped back behind the door again, desperate for a barrier between them. Something to keep him from reaching out and pulling her inside the room. He was close. Too close. The hunger pushed and pulled inside of him and he knew he wouldn't last five seconds if she kept looking at him with such passion in her eyes. And he had to last. He didn't do sex. And he certainly didn't do it with the locals.

Then again, she wasn't actually a local. She was temporary. In town in search of her ex. Or so she said.

She was lying. Even more, she was good at lying, at masking her feelings, which made him all the more suspicious of her. She wasn't who she pretended to be.

Not that it mattered.

Regardless of who she was or why she was here, she wasn't from Skull Creek. She was temporary. She wouldn't be hanging around next week. Or next month. Or next year. And he wouldn't have to face her again should he come back and visit Cody. So why shouldn't he take her up on what she was so obviously offering?

At the same time, there was just something about her that made him wary. The fact that she wasn't easily influenced by him bothered him to no end. He couldn't bend her to his will, otherwise she would turn and walk away right now.

Walk.

He stared deep into her eyes and sent the silent command, but she simply batted her eyelashes, her gaze hopeful, hungry.

She was stronger than any other woman he'd ever known. Different. Dangerous.

To his resolve. His peace of mind. His heart.

When the last thought struck, he drop-kicked it back out. That was the last thing he had to worry about. He didn't stick around long enough for his heart to get involved. He kept his distance and took his sustenance only when he needed it.

His dick throbbed, reminding him that the one thing he needed right now was a warm, lush woman.

The woman standing before him.

"I really have to go," he murmured. "I've got someone waiting on me."

"Oh." Disappointment flashed in her gaze and he couldn't help himself.

"My brother," he heard himself blurt. *What the hell?* He didn't explain. Even more, he didn't talk. *Just shut up and let her think the worst. Even more, shut the door right friggin' now before you do something you'll really regret.* "He's getting married next Saturday and tonight's the shower. It's a couples' shower," he explained. "Not that I'm a part of a couple. But it's for men and women and I'm family so I have to go."

"Oh." The disappointment faded in a rush of relief. She smiled. "Where are they getting married?"

"A friend of ours has a ranch outside of town. The wedding is there, but the shower is at Darlington House. It's this old restored mansion over on Main, near the town square. It used to be the home of Sam Black, the founder of Skull Creek, but now it's a historic landmark. They give tours and use it for special events. Weddings. Receptions. Anniversary parties."

"Showers," she added. She smiled and his chest tightened. "What about afterward? We could meet up later." She looked so hopeful that he almost agreed.

Almost.

But Brent had been resisting the lust for sex that burned inside of him far too long to give in so easily. Sex was off limits while he was in Skull Creek. It was a vow he'd made when Cody had asked him to stick around, one he intended to keep. It would be hard enough to leave his brother when all was said and done. He wasn't adding a woman to the list.

"I'm busy later," he murmured. And then he closed the door before he did something really stupid like pull her close, sinking his fangs into her sweet neck and his cock into her warm and willing body.

No sex, he reminded himself. Even more, no blood and sex. That was a double whammy. A sure-fire way to find himself in a heap of trouble.

Having sex with her would be bad enough. But having sex with her *and* drinking her blood? That would tie him to her emotionally. He would be able to hear her thoughts, feel her feelings, *know* her.

No way. No how. *Hell*, no.

Brent listened as her heels clicked back toward her room. The knob clicked. Hinges creaked. The door thudded shut and he welcomed a rush of relief.

But it was short-lived when he realized that all that separated them was measly sheetrock. His hands trembled and his body tightened and he pulled on his clothes with lightning speed. Snatching up his keys and his Stetson, he headed for his car, his gaze locked on the Camaro. He wasn't going to look toward her room. Or think about her and the way she'd looked in her tight red dress and sparkly shoes. Or the fact that he was so hard he could have cut diamonds at the moment.

Getting the hell out of there. That's all that was on his mind at the moment.

That and finding a little relief. No way would he make it fifteen minutes at the shower in his present state. He needed to sate the hunger deep in his belly. He needed calm. And he knew just how to get it.

He fired the engine, pulled out of the parking lot and headed to the Dairy Freeze for a quick bite.

He couldn't do it.

Brent stared at the woman draped over his arm.

The waitress from the other night. Just as willing. Just as eager.

Her heartbeat echoed in his ears, begging for his fangs, but he couldn't seem to make himself do it. As hungry as he was, he wasn't hungry for this. For her.

"Please," she murmured, her gaze glazed with passion as she stared up at him. While she didn't consciously remember, her subconscious did and that's what was in control at the moment. She wanted the sweet release he'd given her the other night when he'd drank from her. The pleasure.

And he wanted Abby.

The truth thrummed through him and he released the woman. Buttoning her blouse back up, he stared deep into her eyes.

This was just another dream. Go back inside and forget all about it. About me.

For a split second, he wished he could turn the mind control on himself. He wanted to forget Abby and the way she'd looked in her red dress. The way she'd looked last night.

Even more, he wanted to forget the way she'd looked at him.

The desperation. The desire.

He'd had women want him before, but only because of what he was. Abby wasn't influenced by that. She was strong. Immune to his control. Unfazed by it.

Yet she still wanted him.

Of her own accord.

That's why he couldn't forget her. And that's why he bypassed the various couples clustered here and there in the main parlor and headed straight for the bar the moment he arrived at Darlington House.

"What's up with you?" Cody asked him when he cornered him later that night.

"I'm just having a drink."

"You don't drink. We don't drink." Vampires were more sensitive, which meant they not only saw and heard things that most people couldn't. They also felt things more intensely. Translation? Brent was a cheap drunk.

Usually.

Oddly enough, three glasses of Crown Royal still hadn't been enough to make Brent forget Abby and her sexy red dress.

"Slow down," Cody told him when he tossed down number four.

"Shouldn't you be helping your bride-to-be open gifts?" He motioned to Miranda who stood across the room, holding up yet another silver serving platter. "Don't these people realize you can't use that?"

"Some are humans and no, they don't realize it.

And they'd better not realize it." He gave Brent a warning look. "Take it easy, okay?"

"No problem." He waved the waiter off when he started to refill the glass and Cody looked relieved.

"So what did you think about the house?" When Brent tried to look puzzled, Cody grinned. "I know you stopped by. Nice, huh?"

"It's a house."

"Do you think she'll like it?"

"I think you should stop worrying about whether she likes it and start worrying over what you're going to do with seven Crockpots."

Cody glanced behind him in time to see Miranda unwrap the next present and his face fell. "Whatever happened to gift cards?" he muttered as he made his way back over to his fiancée.

Brent pushed away from the bar, said his goodbyes and slipped out before Cody got to the envelope he'd left on the table upon his arrival. Outside, he climbed into his car, hiked the windows down and spent the next half hour hauling ass down the interstate, feeling the wind whip at his skin. Hoping it would cool him down and ease the lust eating away inside of him.

No such luck.

He was still as hot, as horny as ever when he pulled into the parking lot later that night.

He killed the engine and sat there, staring through

the windshield at the closed curtains of her room. He knew he should go out to Cody's. He could sleep in his brother's basement tonight and save himself a night of tossing and turning and fantasizing.

At least that's what he told himself.

But deep down, he knew he was past the point of sleep. She was in his head, under his skin, and there was no escaping the picture she'd made on the bed with her legs spread, or on his doorstep wearing a racy red dress and eager smile.

It was crazy, but he couldn't decide which he liked better. He knew it should be the first, but as much as he'd liked seeing her naked body, he'd liked seeing her smile, too. The tilt of her full lips. The flash of uncertainty in her gaze, as if she wasn't half as daring as she pretended to be.

She wasn't, despite the fact that she'd pulled the curtains aside and was now standing in the window, staring at him.

Drive away.

The command echoed, but damned if he could make himself start the engine. Instead, he sat still and waited to see what she would do next.

11

HE'D TURNED HER DOWN.

The knowledge should have been enough to sway Abby from her current plan, but it wasn't.

She hadn't made it through boot camp and years of special training by being easily discouraged. When she made up her mind to do something, she did it.

Now was no different.

While Brent had turned her down, he hadn't wanted to turn her down. He'd wanted to reach out, pull her into his arms and kiss her senseless. She'd seen as much in the stiff set of his muscles. The flare of desire in his eyes. The tense set to his jaw. He'd wanted her, but he'd held back.

He was holding back now.

She watched as he sat behind the steering wheel,

his hands clenching the wheel, as if he couldn't quite decide what to do.

While he might not be able to make up his mind, she'd already made up hers. If putting on a sexy outfit hadn't been enough to push him past the point of no return, she would just have to try taking it off.

Slowly.

She leaned over and flipped on the ancient radio that sat on a nearby table. A turn of the knob and she cleared away the static and tuned in to a local country station. A twangy, sexy Big and Rich song filled her ears and she closed her eyes. The beat filled her head and thrummed through her body. She started to move her hips from side to side. Pushing her arms into the air, she slid her hands beneath her hair and lifted the weight, the same way she'd seen Winona demonstrate during her pole dancing snippet.

The realization that Brent was parked outside, watching her from his car made her heart pound and her blood race. Her body came alive, her nerves buzzing, and her movements grew more seductive as she listened to the lyrics about saving horses and riding cowboys.

She danced for the next few seconds, lost in the rhythm of the song and the seductive edge, until the music finally faded into a slow tune by Faith Hill and Tim McGraw.

Chancing a peek to see if Brent was still watching, she found the car empty. Disappointment rushed through her as she came to a dead stop and stared through the window. And then came the insecurity.

Maybe she'd read him wrong. Heaven knew it wouldn't be the first time. She'd been so convinced that Hockey Hunk had returned her feelings, so dead set in the notion that he loved her as desperately as she loved him that she'd poured out her feelings that night only to have them thrown back into her face.

There'd been no feelings involved now. Just lust. And pride.

She was such an idiot.

Then and now.

"Don't stop on my account." The deep, sultry voice brought her whirling around to find Brent standing in the corner of the room. His eyes gleamed. Tension held his body tight. His muscles bunched beneath his white T-shirt. Taut lines carved his face, making him seem harsh, fierce, predatory.

She glanced at the closed door. She hadn't heard it open. No footsteps. Nothing. It was as if he'd slid through the keyhole. "How did you get in here—" she started, but then he was right in front of her, his fingertip pressed to her lips.

"Don't talk," he murmured. "Just finish what you started."

Suddenly the specifics of how he'd gotten into her room ceased to matter. The only important thing was that he was there. Right in front of her. Watching again.

Waiting.

She licked her lips and touched a finger to her throat, to the frantic pounding of her pulse. Her hand lingered before she slid a finger to the edge of her dress, tracing the line where warm flesh met spandex before moving to the spaghetti strap.

Hooking her finger beneath, she slid the stretchy material down over her shoulder. She did the same with the other strap until the material caught only on her aroused nipples. She traced the indentation of one, fingering the peak until a gasp trembled from her lips.

Brent watched, his eyes dark and hooded and bright, bright blue—

Wait a second.

He didn't have blue eyes. He had green eyes. Vivid, grass-green eyes that made her think of lazy summer days and endless stretches of pasture. She blinked and sure enough, his eyes were green again.

Again? They were always green. You're so worked up that you're not thinking straight.

And how. Her hands trembled. Her body shook.

"More," he murmured, the one word throaty and raw and desperate.

A surge of feminine power went through her and she pushed the material down over her aroused nipples, to her waist. She eased it over her hips, her thighs, her knees, until it puddled around her ankles.

Leaning down, she grasped the edge of the dress and tried to step free. Her heel caught and she stumbled backward.

"Easy." Brent caught her, his strong, powerful hands steady on her arms.

Heat rushed to her cheeks, but he didn't seem the least put off by her clumsiness. His gaze smoldered. His touch lingered for a long moment, as if he hated to let her go.

He did.

He forced his hands away and stepped back to give her the floor again.

She drew a deep, shaky breath and watched the flare of desire in his eyes when her breasts lifted up and out. The sight fed her confidence and she reached for her front bra clasp. A twist of her fingers and the cups fell aside. Cool air slid over her bare breasts, but then his gaze chased away the sudden chill as quickly as it had come. Her heart pounded harder. Her blood rushed faster.

Just like that, a drop of sweat slid down her temple. She was hot. A feeling that had nothing to do with the failing air conditioner and everything to do with the fire that burned between them.

She touched the undersides of her breasts, cupping the soft mounds, weighing them and feeling the heat of her own touch for a long, delicious moment. All the while, she imagined that it was Brent touching her, searing her.

She skimmed her palms over her nipples, down the plane of her stomach, to the waistband of her panties. The moment she felt the soft cotton, doubt pushed past the desire drumming at her temples. She wore plain regulation panties without a hint of lace. No sequins. No beading. Nothing even remotely sexy.

When she'd bought the new clothes, why oh why hadn't she opted for new undies, too?

Because while she was, indeed, female, she didn't think like one. She thought in terms of comfort rather than appearance. Functionality rather than seduction.

Brent Braddock didn't seem to notice. He stared at her as if she wore the skimpiest thong. His gaze gleamed with excitement. Desperation. Hunger.

Impatience rushed through her, chasing away the insecurity and filling her with pure, raw need. A need she had to satisfy or else.

She pushed the panties down and toed them to the side. When she leaned down to work at the straps of the shoe, Brent's voice stopped her.

"Leave them on. They're sexy."

You're sexy.

His deep voice echoed in her head, but she didn't see his lips move. Before she could wonder about it, he leaned down and touched his lips to hers in a quick, hungry kiss that sent electricity zinging from the point of contact.

The sensation ended all too soon and he pulled away. Then he simply stood there. Staring at her. Waiting for more.

She quickly obliged. She touched the tip of one breast and circled before moving to the other. She rubbed her nipple and squeezed, making her own breath catch before she moved lower, over her belly button, her pelvis, to the damp, swollen flesh between her legs. She stroked herself and her nerves hummed. Another lingering stroke and she pushed deep inside her drenched flesh.

Pressure gripped her, so sweet and intense, and she gasped. She'd pleasured herself many times before, but it had never felt the way it did now. With Brent so close. So interested.

She fanned her fingers, pushing and wiggling until her body swayed from the desire gripping her.

But it wasn't enough. She wanted his fingers inside of her. His touch. Him.

And he wanted her.

"Just sex," he murmured, his gaze suddenly wary. "That's all this is. I don't want to date you or get to know you or listen to your life story. I'm not looking for a relationship."

"Neither am I." She closed the few inches that separated them. Staring up into his heated gaze, she murmured, "Your turn."

He hesitated a split-second and she feared he would turn and walk away, the way he'd done last night. And today.

Not this time.

Instead, he reached out and rasped one nipple with his knuckle. Pleasure bolted through her and she caught a gasp that bubbled from her lips.

He slid his arms around her and down the small of her back until he cupped her buttocks. As if she weighed nothing, he pulled her legs up on either side of him and lifted her. He settled her firmly against the rock-hard length barely contained by his zipper.

She wrapped her arms around his neck and lost herself to the delicious friction as he rocked her. The course material of his jeans rasped against her sensitive flesh, and pleasure rushed through her, igniting every nerve ending until her body glowed from the feel of his.

A day's growth of beard rubbed against the tender flesh of her neck, the slope of her breasts, chafing her and stirring her sensitive skin. He arched her backward, drew one swollen nipple into his mouth and sucked her so hard she almost fainted from the pleasure.

The sensation was both pleasure and pain as he suckled and nipped with his teeth. No man had ever done that and she arched as warmth gushed between her legs from the pure intensity.

Then he captured her lips in a kiss that sent her senses reeling. His tongue tangled with hers, delving and tasting until she could barely breathe.

He turned and she felt the mattress at her back. He leaned back and made quick work of his jeans until he stood before her wearing nothing but a look of pure intent.

She leaned up on her elbows as her gaze swept him from head to toe. Muscles carved his torso, from his bulging biceps and shoulders to his ripped abdomen. Dark, silky hair sprinkled his chest, narrowing to a tiny whorl of silk that bisected his abs before spreading into a soft nest that circled his sizeable erection. A drop of pearly liquid beaded on the plum-like head of his penis and she had the insane urge to lean forward and taste him.

Before she had the chance, he turned and retrieved a condom from his pocket.

He tore open the foil packet and rolled it down his hard length. Catching her bent knees in his hands, he parted her and gazed at the heart of her.

No man had ever looked at her so fiercely, so intently and a wave of doubt spiraled through her. She tried to close her legs.

"Don't be shy now. Not with me." His gaze caught and held hers. "Not ever with me."

She nodded and let herself open. He looked his fill, his gaze roving over her, his eyes flaring so hot and bright that she felt her own body temperature rise.

When she was this close to going up in flames, he leaned over her and plunged his hard, hot length inside, until flesh met flesh and he filled her completely.

The feeling took her breath away and her heart stopped for a long moment. She'd never felt as close to a man before.

Sure, she'd had sex. But it had always been swift and to the point. The primary goal? To get to the good stuff. The orgasm itself.

This was different. This *was* the good stuff. His

body flush against hers. His lips driving her insane. His hands roaming over her body. His erection rasping her tender insides.

He pushed himself an inch deeper before he started to withdraw. She clutched at his shoulders, desperate for more as he plunged back inside. In and out. Over and over. Until her nerves spun out of control.

Sensation snatched her up and whirled her around like a tornado. The air rushed from her lungs and the room started to spin.

He pushed deeper, harder, faster, until she couldn't take anymore. Pleasure crashed over her, turning her this way and that, spinning her faster than she'd ever thought possible in her wildest, most erotic fantasies.

This *was* a fantasy, she reminded herself even though it felt so incredibly real. The roughness of his skin, the power of his body, the possessiveness as he stared down at her and bucked into her one final time.

His back arched, his muscles strained. His eyes glittered, blazing a bright, brilliant purple—

She blinked and the vivid color faded into a sea of sparkling green. Confusion rushed through her, but then he rolled onto his back and pulled her flush against his side. His arms went around her and he held her tight, as if she were his one and only. His woman. And he never meant to let her go.

It was a crazy, hopelessly romantic thought. The kind straight out of a cheesy romance novel, but then that's what this was.

A fairytale.

A fantasy.

One that would end all too quickly once Rayne arrived in Skull Creek and she returned to her life.

It would be over all too soon, which was why she intended to relish every moment of what was happening right now.

She closed her eyes and snuggled deeper into his embrace.

12

WHAT THE HELL was he doing?

Not the sex part, of course. He knew why he'd done that. The moment he'd seen her dancing in the window, he'd known he couldn't resist any longer. Even more, he hadn't wanted to resist. While he'd yet to figure out Abby, he'd learned enough to know that she wasn't like one of the locals. There would be no seeing her day in and day out.

And since she was the only woman he couldn't read, he knew there would be no getting to know her. No real connection.

Just sex.

It made sense, which was why he'd given in last night.

That and one too many drinks.

So he didn't regret the sex part. It had been fantastic. Phenomenal.

It was the fact that she was curled up next to him sleeping like a baby that he was having trouble with.

That, and the fact that he liked it.

A helluva lot.

The realization struck and he stiffened. He slid away from her and threw his legs over the side of the bed. He was a vampire, for Christ's sake. He didn't cuddle. He had sex and drank blood and inspired fear in the heart of millions. He wasn't the cuddling type, and neither was she. He could tell by the way she rolled onto her back and threw her arms above her head that she wasn't used to sleeping with anyone.

Yet she'd fallen asleep in *his* arms as if it were the most natural thing in the world. As if she liked it. As if she liked him.

He ditched the thought. There was no *like* involved at all. They barely knew each other. He'd worn her out, soaked up her delicious energy. It made sense she would be exhausted to the point of falling asleep.

What didn't make sense was the fact that he still wanted her. He should have felt one hundred percent satisfied, his hunger sated.

He wasn't.

Staring at her spread out on the sheets, he wanted more than anything to climb back into bed with her. He wanted to see if she made the same noises if he licked her to the point of orgasm. If she would cry his name at the moment of release. If she would bury her head in his neck and fall fast asleep when they were done.

Crazy.

Sleeping wasn't on the list of possibilities with Abby. Nor was waking up with her or having breakfast or waltzing outside hand-in-hand in the bright light of day.

There was no morning after for Brent. He was a vampire, and so he gathered up his clothes and did what he'd been doing for the past one hundred and something years.

He turned his back and walked away.

ABBY LISTENED to the click of the door and the roar of his engine.

He was leaving.

That fact shouldn't have bothered her.

For one thing, she hated sleeping with anyone. She was a major bed hog and so it was better that he'd left before she'd had to fight him for the covers. Besides, sleeping wasn't part of her fantasy. It was all about unleashing her feminine wiles and she'd done so last night. Now it was time to get some much needed rest.

Then she could go for round two tonight.

And that was the problem in a nutshell.

She much preferred Brent not sticking around to see her in the bright light of day with major bedhead. Talk about blowing her newly found image.

At the same time, she wasn't nearly done building that image of herself as a desirable woman. She had several days left until Rayne came back and she had to return to her life, and she wanted to make the most of each. She certainly wasn't bummed because she'd thought for a split-second that Brent might actually like her. They didn't even know each other, and she fully intended to keep it that way.

No, it was time to move on. If she wanted to unleash her feminine side, she didn't have to do it with him.

There were plenty of men in Skull Creek. Granted, she might not have the same sizzling chemistry with any other man, but she was willing to give it a shot and test out a few more tidbits of wisdom courtesy of Winona and her infomercials.

Like the fact that men had a weakness for feet.

That's what Winona preached when Abby turned on the television set later that morning.

"Get a pedicure," the old woman was saying. "Clean up those tootsies and, if you're lucky, your man might take the hint and suck on a few."

It made sense and so Abby headed for the local hair salon to indulge in her first ever pedicure.

Because this fantasy wasn't about Brent. It was about Abby. About delving deep and living out her most erotic thoughts. It was about enjoying her femininity.

Even if it hurt like hell.

"Do you have to scrub so hard?" she asked the blonde who leaned over the footrest, a pumice stone in her hand and a determined look on her face.

"What on earth did you do? Walk across the Sahara barefoot? Your feet are as rough as horse hooves."

"Thanks for the boost to my confidence."

"Seriously. Haven't you ever heard of lotion?"

"I don't usually have time for lotion." Not in the military. She barely had time to snag a tube of Chapstick at the commissary in between field operations.

Until now.

She had five full days left to herself before the real world intruded. "I'd like a foot bath, too," she told the blonde. "And a paraffin wax. And a hot oil massage on the balls of my feet."

By the time she left the salon, she'd spent a hundred and fifty dollars and her feet looked ready for a flip flop commercial.

Instead of heading for the beach though, she hit the nearest bar and grill, determined to make the most of the time she had left. She wore a blue jean mini skirt, a white tank top with the phrase *Cowgirls Do It Better* spelled out in pink rhinestones and a pair of pink high heels.

Her outfit wasn't as flashy as the red dress last night, but it did spark some serious interest from the male clientale of Joe's Bar and Grill. A truth that fed her self-esteem and kept her from running back to the motel to see if Brent had returned.

This wasn't about turning on one man. It was about exercising her newfound feminine wiles and wowing them all.

And that's exactly what she intended to do.

SHE WASN'T IN her room.

Brent pulled into the parking lot and stared at the darkened window where Abby had put on her show the night before. Disappointment rushed through him. It was a crazy feeling because he surely hadn't expected her to be ready and waiting for him after he'd walked out on her this morning.

Any other woman, yes.

They would have been ready and waiting for him, desperate for a little more of his attention.

Not Abby. She wasn't the least bit fazed by his

vampire charisma. No sitting around, pining away. No meeting him at the door wearing nothing but Saran Wrap and a hopeful expression.

Instead, she was prowling the local bar.

The truth hit him when he turned the corner and saw her rental car parked in front of a neon Bud Light sign. It was a cause for celebration, right? The last thing he wanted was a woman getting hooked on him. But damned if he wasn't a little ticked off that she'd moved on quite so fast.

He frowned and an image rushed at him. He saw Abby stretched out on the bed, a smile curving her full lips as she reached out for another man.

Was she friggin' nuts?

His spot wasn't even cold and she was already looking for a replacement? Not that she would find one. Hell, no. What they had done last night had been one-of-a-kind. An experience she wouldn't be able to duplicate with just anyone.

On top of that, she wasn't the type of woman to sleep around. She wasn't nearly experienced enough to tell the good guys from the bad.

And you know this because…?

He'd seen the hesitation in her eyes, the awkwardness of her moves and the damned wonder on her face when she'd exploded around him. She wasn't nearly the wild and wicked woman she pretended to be and she was about to bite off more than she could chew if he didn't stop her.

He pulled up behind her, killed the engine and climbed out of the car.

"So you're from Charlotte?"

"Chicago," she told the cowboy sitting next to her. His name was Paul and he was more the drugstore variety than the real deal. He sold real estate during the day and bootscooted his way across the local honky tonks at night. He'd been on his way to the Cherry Creek Saloon when he'd decided to stop off for a drink. One look at Abby and he'd settled on the stool next to her and offered to buy her a drink.

She was on her second and doing her best not to notice the narrowness of his shoulders beneath the starched shirt. So what if he wasn't as muscular as Brent? He was still a decent guy. Even if he did smell like the fragrance section of a department store.

"So you've been in Skull Creek for two months now?" he asked.

"Two days."

"Oh, yeah." He grinned. "I knew that."

He did. She'd told him as much three times, along with the fact that she was from Chicago and she liked Italian food and her favorite color was red. But he'd been too distracted by her chest to pay much attention to anything she said.

Yeah, baby.

She'd wowed him to the point that he couldn't think straight, much less pay attention to what she was saying.

Score one for Abby the ultra femme.

At the same time, it would have been kind of nice if he had looked her in the eyes. At least once.

"That's a really nice shirt."

"You should know, buddy" came a deep, familiar voice. "You've been staring at it long enough."

Awareness sizzled up Abby's spine and she knew, even before she chanced a glance, that Brent Braddock stood directly behind her.

13

ABBY TWISTED TO SEE Brent, his gaze riveted on a surprised Paul. The cowboy's hat bobbed as he forced his attention from Abby's chest to the man standing behind her.

"Who are you?" Paul asked.

"Her bodyguard. Now get lost."

"But I coughed up the cash for two margaritas."

"You'll be coughing up your dinner if you don't slide off that barstool and start walking."

Brent didn't have to repeat himself. Paul hit his boots and retreated across the room to a redhead who stood near the jukebox. Strong fingers gripped Abby's arm and tugged her from her seat.

She shrugged away from Brent and faced off with him, her chin in the air. Her chest heaved from all the extra air she was forced to draw in because suddenly, she couldn't seem to get enough with him so close. "What are you doing?"

"Saving you from yourself."

"Thanks, but no thanks. I don't need a white knight."

"Do you know what that guy had in mind?"

She arched an eyebrow. "Sex?"

"Sex," he declared. She smiled and his gaze narrowed. "What are you? Some kind of nympho?"

"I'm a jilted woman who's trying to get over a bad relationship and have a little fun. I've got a week until my ex rolls back into town so I can tie up loose ends. I want to enjoy myself until then."

She could feel his gaze on her for a long moment. "Bullshit," he finally muttered.

"What's that supposed to mean?"

"It means that you're not a receptionist and you're not from Chicago and you sure as hell aren't trying to get over your ex."

"How do you know?"

He picked up the Driver's License sitting on the bar next to her margarita, which she'd handed over when she'd ordered. "Because this was issued in South Carolina, not Illinois."

"So? Maybe I spent most of my life in South Carolina and moved to Chicago just recently."

"Did you?"

"I thought you didn't want to know?" she countered. "Not me or my life history. Just sex, remember?"

He looked like he wanted to say something, but then his mouth clamped together and he signaled the waiter for a beer.

"So what's with Urban Cowboy over there? He doesn't seem like your type."

"You don't know my type. You don't know me," she reminded him.

He didn't say anything for a long moment. Instead, his gaze moved around the room, touching here and there, before zeroing in on her once again. "I know that guy lives with his mother and bums money off her to buy beer." When she arched an eyebrow, he shrugged. "It's a small town."

"Thanks for the warning, but I hadn't planned on marrying him. It's all about fun, remember. A week of it, to be exact." She still had five days left. A lifetime compared to her usual schedule.

A piddly amount when it came to the rest of her life.

She had to build enough memories to last. It was a realization she'd come to during her foot fest that day. Odds were she would never get the chance she had right now. No time to play dress up. To pretend to be something she wasn't. A lifetime and this was the first time she could really and truly enjoy herself. Once she dragged Rayne back to face charges and cleared her reputation, she would go back to doing what she did best—leading her men and running successful field ops.

In the meantime, she was going to make the most of her time in Skull Creek.

With or without Brent.

She glanced to the side and eyed him. He looked so handsome that she wanted to hop into his lap and do her own variation of the very detailed lap dance she'd seen Winona demonstrate. It was a wild, crazy impulse. One she never would have acted on in the real world.

She didn't act on it now, not with him sitting so close and staring at her as if she'd been caught with her hand in the cookie jar. He looked irritated. Jealous even and guilt spiraled through her.

Make-believe, she reminded herself. None of this was real. Not his concerned look or the strange possessiveness gleaming in his gaze.

But for a few seconds as they sat side by side, his thigh warm and strong against hers, it felt real. *He* felt real.

"You should be careful," he finally said. "You can't just go around picking up men. It's dangerous."

"Trust me, I can take care of myself."

"So sayeth every woman."

"I'm serious. I've got a black belt in Karate and years of hand-to-hand combat training," she blurted before she could stop herself. When he arched an eyebrow, she added, "My dad was career military. He taught me everything he knew." Martial Arts. Special Weapons. She could even arm wrestle.

Not that she told Brent that. She'd already admitted too much and he'd been more than clear that he didn't care.

But for someone who didn't give a crap he was being awfully nosy. The realization made her want to smile.

Silence settled around them as she sipped her margarita. His thigh brushed hers and her heart stuttered. So much for moving on to the next guy.

She still wanted this one. She just wasn't so sure he still wanted her. He was here, which said a lot. At the same time, he was also griping her out which didn't exactly spell out I-want-to-jump-your-bones.

"What branch of the Armed Forces is your dad in?" he asked after several seconds of silence ticked by. It was the last thing she expected from him. At the same time, he seemed eager for a distraction from the heat flowing between them.

She eyed him. "Are you sure you want to hear this?"

"No, but tell me anyway." *It's better than sitting here wondering how I'm going to keep my hands off you.*

The words whispered through her head and she couldn't help herself. She smiled.

Not because he'd actually said them. She knew it had to be her imagination at work. His lips hadn't so much as moved. At the same time, she had the strangest feeling that the ridiculous thought rang true.

"*Was.* He was a Navy recruiter. He passed away a few years ago from a heart attack."

"I'm sorry."

"Don't be. He died doing what he loved most— briefing new recruits."

He grinned and the pain that she always felt when she talked about her dad eased just a little. "Actually, he didn't die right away." She wasn't sure why she was telling him this. He hadn't asked and even if he had, she never talked about it. Not in the few years since he'd passed away and certainly not now, to a virtual stranger.

But he didn't feel like a stranger. There was something familiar about him. While she didn't know him from Adam, she had the absurd notion that he understood.

That he understood her loss because he'd faced his own.

"They took him to the hospital, but he didn't want to call me. He wasn't a very emotional man. I busted out crying when I scraped my knee once and he had a fit. Crying is for the weak and Trentons aren't weak, he always used to say. That was the first and last time I ever cried. I didn't even cry when they handed me his ashes. I should have." Her gaze riveted on a small drop of condensation that slid down the outside of her glass. "I should have cried, right?" The words tumbled past her lips. The accusation she'd felt every moment of every day. The sneaking suspicion that haunted her and reminded her that she was every bit the cold, emotionless person her father had once been. "Most people cry when they lose their dad." Except the cold, heartless ones.

"Trentons don't cry," her father had said. *"They don't show weakness and they don't act silly over some boy and they don't jeopardize their entire future to go to some silly prom. Suck it up, girl. You're a Trenton."*

And so she had. She'd sucked it up and buried her feelings to the point that she'd stopped thinking she even had any. And then her father had died, and his death had proved as much.

"My father always wanted me to be tough. I guess he finally got his wish."

"He doesn't sound like much of a father."

"He wasn't. He was strict and demanding and I think he always blamed me for my mother's death. She died when I was a few months old. She had diabetes and having me put too much of a strain on her system."

"It wasn't your fault."

She'd told herself as much many times in the past, but hearing him say it made her actually believe it.

"I lost my mother in a fire."

"And your dad?"

"I don't know. He left long before that and never looked back. It was just me and my brothers after that."

"How many brothers?"

When he hesitated, she added, "Come on. We're only talking. I promise I won't hold it against you later."

He arched an eyebrow. "Just sex?"

"Just great sex."

He grinned. "Three."

"I always wondered what it would be like to have brothers."

"You wouldn't be sitting here right now, that's for sure. No brother would stand by while his sister cruised a bar for strange men."

"Is that how you see me? Like a sister?"

"You're not my sister." His gaze caught and held

hers, as if he knew she needed to hear the words. "Not by a long shot."

Silence stretched between them once again, but it wasn't awkward this time. A sense of camaraderie wound between them, crossing the distance and killing the tension. A feeling that fed her courage and urged her to voice the one thought playing in her head. "You're right about me, you know."

"I'm always right, sugar."

A grin tugged at her lips before the expression faded into one of serious intent. "I don't do one night stands, but I meant it when I said I want to spend the next five days having some serious fun. Since we have great chemistry, it makes sense to have fun with you instead of bringing home a different cowboy every night. It would be just physical, of course. I'm really not looking for a relationship." Her gaze met his. "So how about it? Are you up for a repeat of last night?"

"Hardly." She frowned and a grin tugged at the corner of his mouth. "I was hoping it would be even better."

And then he grabbed her hand and led her out of the bar.

WHEN THEY ARRIVED back at the motel, Abby didn't waste any time on small talk. True to her word, she kept things strictly physical and stripped off her clothes. Once she'd shed everything, she reached for his T-shirt.

He lifted his arms and let her slide the cotton over his head. She backed him toward the bed then until the backs of his knees hit the mattress and he sat down on the edge.

Then she dropped to her knees and wedged herself between his legs as she leaned forward. Her lips closed over his right nipple. Her teeth caught him, her tongue flicking out to ply the nub.

"Holy hell," he ground out, his gaze fixed on her head as she suckled him. Her body wedged closer, pressing against his massive hard-on and his gut tightened. His pulse raced and he had the sudden image of her trailing her lips lower, unzipping his pants and taking him into her mouth.

Her moist red lips pressed against his skin and stirred the hunger. He could feel the need bubbling inside of her. He threaded his fingers through her hair, holding her close and soaking up the sweet heat.

But there was more. He felt his own lust building until he wanted nothing more than to haul her into his lap, press her back against the mattress and devour her ripe nipples. He wanted to spread her legs.

To slide into her. To sink his fangs into her sweet, delectable neck.

He wouldn't.

This was sex, he reminded himself, determined to stay focused. Even more, this was her show. He'd taken the lead last night, but it was her turn now.

She pulled back and stared up at him with heavy-lidded eyes. "Do you like that?"

He nodded and her slim fingers reached out to unfasten his jeans. "Do you like this?" Her knuckles grazed him as she worked the zipper over his hard length. His entire body trembled in anticipation. He tilted up just enough to let her pull his jeans and underwear down to his hips.

His penis jutted forward. The veins bulged, the skin slick and tight. A white drop beaded on the head and her gaze riveted on it. She licked at her bottom lip once, twice, and then she leaned forward. Her tongue flicked out and she lapped at his essence.

Electricity zapped him and his nerves started to tingle. She licked him from root to tip, making him burn hotter before drawing him into the wet heat of her mouth.

He closed his eyes as hunger sucker-punched him in the gut. His jaw ached and his fangs tingled. He knew she would see the truth if she glanced up at him and so he cradled her head, urging her to continue even though her mouth was pure torture.

He needed her to stop, but he couldn't stop her.

He didn't want to.

Pleasure drenched his body and he braced himself against coming right then and there. It wasn't about his own orgasm. That wasn't how it worked. He was the one who fed off of *her* excitement, her ecstasy. He didn't even have to come to feel satisfied.

But he wanted to.

He gathered his composure and forced his eyes open. Her silky hair trailed over his lap and he reached down, pushing the soft strands back so that he could see her face. He meant to pull her away, but he couldn't help himself. He watched as her red lips slid over his hard length. She suckled him, swirling her tongue around and around, pushing him closer to the brink. So close—

With a growl, he cupped her face and pushed her away. Her confused gaze collided with his. "Did I do something wrong?"

It was the perfect opportunity to kill the heat between them and say "Yes, you're not any good at oral sex."

But he couldn't bring himself to lie. Not with her looking so uncertain and so damned beautiful.

"You did everything just right." Satisfaction

beamed in her gaze and filled him with a strange sense of warmth.

She slid up his body and touched her lips to his.

He tasted his own essence and it stirred the beast that lived and breathed inside of him. His tongue tangled with hers and he deepened the kiss, wanting to consume her the way she'd consumed him only a few moments ago. The kiss was hot and wet and mesmerizing. So much more than ever before.

Because she was so much more.

He pushed aside the startling thought and reached for her hips, pulling her down onto his lap, and urging her legs up on either side of him.

He cupped her bottom and plunged into her slick flesh. Fire shot through him and thunder pounded in his ears. Finally her soft voice pushed past his sensual haze and he became aware of her hand splayed against his chest.

"We need protection," she breathed.

He wanted to tell her that he couldn't hurt her. That he would never hurt her because of what he was. But he'd vowed never to reveal himself to anyone ever again.

Keep quiet and keep moving. That had been his motto since Lila had turned on him.

Never again would he make that same mistake.

No matter how much he suddenly wanted to.

He withdrew and reached for his pants. A few seconds later, he retrieved a foil packet.

She took it from him, pulled out the contents and reached down between them. Her fingers brushed and stroked as she slid the condom over his throbbing length. And then she braced her hands against his chest and drew him deep into her body with one swift, downward motion.

The pleasure was so intense that a groan rumbled from deep in his throat. His entire body went rigid and he clenched his teeth to keep from closing his mouth over her neck and sinking his fangs into her as deep as his cock.

"Don't move." He held onto her sweet ass, his fingers pressing into her softness as he held her still and tried to gather his wits.

He had to think.

To stay in control.

He intended to, but then she arched her back, drawing him in deeper, and shot his intentions to hell and back. Pure pleasure washed over him and need pumped through his veins.

It was a feeling that intensified as she started to ride him, her body clasping his as she moved up and down, side to side. He braced his thighs, holding himself rigid as he massaged her buttocks and pressed hungry kisses to her throat. Her pulse beat against his lips and his throat went dry. His jaw ached.

He took every downward thrust, and met her with an upward plunge. Harder. Faster. Until she reached her breaking point. Her forehead wrinkled and her cheeks flushed and her lips parted. Her fingers dug into his shoulders.

He caught her fierce cry with his mouth and gathered her close as she shook, her climax crashing over her, drenching her and flowing into him from every point of contact. His cock deep inside her. His arms locked tight. Their bodies flush together.

Energy sizzled along his nerve endings and suddenly it was too much. He exploded, his own cry echoing in his ears, along with the frantic beat of her heart. His back arched and his vision clouded a bright brilliant purple.

Her gasp drew his attention and he realized all too late that she was staring smack dab at him. Into him. Shock twisted her features, but there was something else, as well. A strange sense of wonder that killed any fear and kept her gaze locked with his.

She stared at him, seeing him for what he was and the truth crystallized at that moment. Abby Trenton didn't just pose a threat to his existence.

With her sweet smile and her freckled nose and

her stubborn attitude, she posed a major threat to his heart. He'd never met a woman like her before.

And he never would again.

He knew it as he stared into her gaze. He also knew that he was falling in love with her and there wasn't a damned thing he could do to stop it.

14

SHE STARED AT HIM a moment longer before reality seemed to sink in and her eyes went wide. Fear rushed through her and blazed bright in her eyes. Suddenly, Brent forgot all about love and falling.

She'd seen him.

Holy shit, she'd *seen* him.

But he had an even bigger problem. His hunger stirred. His gut twisted and his body shook. He needed a drink. He needed her.

The truth pounded through his head and sent a rush of panic through him. He broke the contact between them, scrambling away. He stumbled to his feet and staggered backwards. His back came up hard against the opposite wall and he heard the crack of plaster. His stomach clenched and his muscles contorted. His mouth watered and his fangs ached. His gaze riveted on her lush body and an invisible hand tightened around him and squeezed.

Abby watched as Brent's eyes blazed a bright, furious red. His teeth pulled back and his fangs glittered and for a split-second, she wanted to rush over to him and give him what he so obviously needed.

Blood.

Her blood.

Denial rushed through her, along with fear. Not the fear of him, but of herself, her reaction. Because for a split second, against the better judgment she'd honed for months in the field, she'd wanted to help him. To reach out. To offer herself.

She still did.

She rushed hell for leather for the bathroom and tried to ignore the ridiculous notion. The door slammed and she flipped the lock.

He was a vampire.

A real, honest-to-goodness *vampire*.

She wouldn't have believed it if she hadn't seen it with her own eyes. Even now, she wasn't one hundred percent certain and her mind raced for a more plausible explanation. The margaritas. She'd had almost three. Translation? She was drunk. Hallucinating. That had to be it.

Why, this entire night was probably just a bad dream. A crazy nightmare wrought from too much alcohol and a lifetime of deprivation when it came to her sexuality. She'd buried her desires far too long and now everything was rushing to the surface, making her punchy and distorting her sense of reality.

That's what it was.

A nightmare.

One she would wake up from all too soon.

"We need to talk." His deep voice slid into her ears, pulling her back to reality and nailing home the truth—this wasn't her imagination. She felt the bare tile beneath her feet, the anxiety pressing down on her. "Please," he added.

So much desperation filled the one word and she almost opened the door. It wasn't a dream. Just a big misunderstanding. There were no such things as vampires. She was having a hallucination. A margarita induced hallucination. The next thing she knew, she would be seeing little green men in sombreros.

"I know this is a lot to grasp."

The air lodged in her chest as shock beat at her already numb brain. She rushed to the sink. Flipping on the faucet, she plunged her hands beneath the cool water and splashed some onto her face, as if she could wash away the images that rolled through her head.

"You're not a vampire," she heard herself say. "There's no such thing."

"There is," he said after a long moment, as if the

words were as hard to say as they were for her to hear. "I know it seems crazy, but it's true."

"A vampire? A real vampire?" She knew she sounded like a raving lunatic repeating herself, but she couldn't help it. She was trying to grasp the impossible and her brain just didn't want to accept it. "Vampires don't exist. Only on TV and in books. Not in real life."

"We exist," he said quietly. "I'm not allergic to garlic and crosses don't bother me, but I'm still a vampire. My senses are heightened and I can do things that most men only dream about. I'm strong and I can hear things. And when I look into someone's eyes I can see what they're thinking, too. Usually..." His voice trailed off for a long moment. "But not with you. For some reason, I can't see into your thoughts. Just the occasional glimpse. You're strong, Abby."

Which explained why she was cowering in the bathroom and clutching the edges of the sink like an idiot.

"I've never met a woman like you. You're different. Special."

It was an admission she'd hoped to hear her entire life. And while the circumstance wasn't one she would have predicted, a rush of satisfaction went through her anyway.

"You're smart and beautiful."

She stared at herself in the bathroom mirror and noted the flush to her cheeks. The sparkle in her eyes. She was different now. She felt it from the tips of her toes to her fingers.

"What did you do to me?"

"Nothing. It's just great sex. That's another perk of being a vampire. I'm pretty good in the sack."

"What else?" she heard herself. This was crazy. She should be crawling out the nearest window and running for help instead of playing twenty questions.

"I can see myself in a mirror like everyone else," he went on. "But that thing about bats is a myth. I can transform into other things if I want to, but it's usually more trouble than it's worth. I can levitate. And I have fangs."

Because he was a vampire. A night stalking, blood-drinking *vampire*.

Her memory raced and suddenly everything started to make sense. The sudden change of his eye color. The way he moved so swiftly and silently. His sudden appearance in her room that first night. His dark good looks and the dangerous pull that seemed to lure her closer against her better judgment.

An image rushed at her and she saw him, his fangs poised, his eyes glowing.

"You were going to bite me, weren't you?"

"I wanted to. I wanted it more than anything, but I wouldn't have done it. I didn't have to. I'd already fed."

"On who?"

"On you, Abby. Vampires don't just feed off of blood. We also crave energy. Sexual energy. Your orgasm fed me enough to curb my bloodlust." Silence settled as she tried to process everything he was saying. "Open the door. I promise I won't hurt you."

She wasn't sure why she believed him except that he'd had plenty of chances to turn her into a human Happy Meal if he'd wanted. The fact that he hadn't echoed through her and suddenly she wanted to flip the lock more than she wanted her next breath.

She wanted to know the truth about him. How long he'd been a vampire, who had turned him and why. She wanted to know everything and that need stirred her fear even more than the fact that he had actual *fangs.*

It was just sex, she reminded herself. She didn't want to know his background. His life. Him.

She just wanted a few wonderful memories to tide her over for the rest of her orderly, routine life.

Emotion push-pulled inside her and she shook her head frantically. This was too much. It was time to stop right now before she did the unthinkable.

She wasn't falling for him. She wasn't falling for anyone, man or vampire.

Never, ever again.

"Get out of here."

"You don't mean that."

"Get out right now before I call the cops."

Silence followed for several long seconds, as if he was trying to decide whether or not to believe her. He shouldn't have. She was bluffing, the same way she'd done time and time again on mission after mission. She knew how to persuade people. To survive.

That's what this was about. Survival. Of her body. Her heart.

Oh, no.

Panic rushed through her and the words tumbled out. "If you don't get out of here, I'm going to scream bloody murder. I mean it."

The thud of a door punctuated her sentence, and just like that he was gone.

She stood there for several long moments listening to the pounding of her own heart before she finally slid the lock aside. Sure enough, the bedroom was empty and a strange sense of loneliness swept over her.

She snatched up her clothes which lay in a heap where she'd left them. Her gaze shifted to Brent's T-shirt that still lay draped over the back of a nearby chair. Before she could stop herself, she reached for the soft cotton and slid it over her head. His scent filled her nostrils and she had the disturbing thought that she'd just lost the one thing that mattered most.

Nuts.

She hardly knew him. And he hardly knew her. They were virtual strangers.

So why did she feel so empty inside?

The question haunted her as she picked her way around the room, snatching up clothing and straightening the covers. Finally when there was nothing left to spend her energy on, she crawled into bed and burrowed beneath the covers.

And then, for the first time since she'd skinned her knee so very long ago, Abby Trenton started to cry.

15

SHE'D SEEN HIM.

She'd really and truly seen him.

Dread and denial whirled together to make his gut ache and his hands tremble. Sure, he knew that she'd glimpsed the truth a time or two when his control had slipped, but it had been so quick that she'd probably written it off as her imagination.

But this time she'd gotten a good, long look.

There were no excuses he could make. No escaping the truth.

He couldn't make her forget. Even though it was a trick of the trade, it didn't work with her. He'd tried it that first night when she'd followed him from the Dairy Freeze and it had been useless. She had a strong will. She knew how to conceal her thoughts and hide behind a mental barrier.

Bottom line, she knew how to keep him out of her head. So he was SOL. He couldn't make her forget all about him.

As depressing as the thought was, he found a small sense of solace in it. For the first time in his life, he didn't want a woman to forget him. He didn't want to blend into the background like a bad dream or vanish in a puff of smoke. He wanted to stand out. To have a permanent place in her memory. In her life.

He ignored the last thought and focused on gunning the engine of his Camaro. He needed to get out of here. To stop thinking and just drive.

He pulled out onto Main Street and headed for the city limits. It was time to pack up and leave. Dillon could text him any information that he might eventually uncover about his sister-in-law's whereabouts.

And Cody?

His brother would just have to get married without him. It wasn't like Brent was going to stand in as his best man. He'd made it clear that he didn't like weddings. Hell, he'd made it clear that he didn't want Cody to get married, period.

Impossible.

It would never work, no matter how much Cody wanted it to. He was too different from Miranda.

And if he turned her?

The possibility stuck in his head. One he'd never

considered because he'd never wanted to doom anyone to his same fate. He'd been a vampire over one hundred and fifty years and he'd never turned anyone.

And he never would.

Especially someone he loved.

It was hard enough living with the pain of rejection. But living with the knowledge that he'd destroyed someone's life? That he'd doomed them to a fate far worse than death?

Not no, but hell no. He wouldn't do it even if Abby begged him.

Not that she would. She feared him. She'd made it perfectly clear that she wanted nothing to do with him. She was probably on the phone at that moment, ranting about vampires and how he'd deceived her. And while he doubted anyone would believe her, particularly after she'd had a few drinks down at the local bar, he knew it was just a matter of time.

He gunned the engine and crossed the railroad tracks at the far edge of town. A turn to his left and he was heading for the Interstate, dead set on getting the hell out of town before people started to get suspicious.

They would. He had no doubt about that.

At the same time, he owed his brother a word of warning. Cody had told him not to get too close, but

Brent hadn't listened. While his gut told him that Abby wouldn't turn on him, he couldn't be sure. Not after the way she'd kicked him out. He picked up his cell phone and dialed.

"Meet me at the new house," he told Cody when his brother picked up on the third ring.

"What's wrong?"

"Just get in the car and drive. Fifteen minutes."

"WHAT'S GOING ON?"

Brent looked at his brother, not knowing quite what to say. "She knows."

"Who knows?"

"Abby."

"Abby who?"

"She's the woman I've been seeing for the past few days. She's new in town. She's here looking for Rayne."

That got Cody's attention. "Why would she be looking for Rayne?"

"She says she's a receptionist, but I think she's military." In fact, he knew she was military after their conversation last night. While she'd played it off as if it were only her background, the pieces had quickly fallen into place.

"We knew it was just a matter of time," Cody said. Rayne had married his sister-in-law a few weeks after being turned into a vampire in the mountains outside of Afghanistan. He'd been attacked and left to fend for himself.

Not knowing what else to do, he'd come home one last time before going on the run from the authorities and himself. He'd been a fledgling vampire. Scared of what he'd become. Fearful that he would hurt someone.

But he'd found a support system right here in Skull Creek with Cody and the handful of other vampires who'd taken up residence in the small town. They'd taught him to control the hunger, to feed it slowly so that it didn't devour him.

Still, the fact that he was coping didn't change the truth—he'd run away from the military and they'd all known it was just a matter of time before someone came looking for him.

They'd all believed it best to meet the threat head on, bending whoever showed up to their will so that they would forget all about Rayne and the fact that he was AWOL.

A plan that might have worked if anyone other than Abby Trenton had shown up.

She was stubborn.

Determined.

Sexy.

The thought struck and he stiffened. It didn't matter how sexy she was. It was over.

He was outta here.

"I'll call the others and see if we can't influence her and send her on her way."

"It won't work."

"How do you know?"

"Because I know. She's got a strong will and she's not easily influenced."

"She can't be that strong."

"Trust me, I've tried. She's not like everyone else. She won't bend. She's got the tenacity of a pit bull. No matter how much I stare into her eyes, I can't get her to listen to me."

Cody didn't say anything. He just stared at Brent long and hard before his face cracked into a smile and he started to laugh.

"What's wrong with you? Didn't you hear anything I said? She knows and she's going to blow the whistle on all of us. There's no way you can win in this situation. She's too stubborn."

"You're falling for her," Cody finally said once his laughter had died down. "Hook, line and sinker."

"Bullshit." There was no *falling* involved. He'd already fallen. Hard.

"You sure as hell are. She's gotten to you."

"She's going to tell the world we're vampires, little

brother. If you have half a brain you'll get the hell out of here before she does."

"I'm not leaving," Cody said after a long contemplative moment. "This is my home now. I won't give it up."

"You're crazy." Brent turned and started for his car.

"And you're scared."

The comment brought him to a dead stop. He turned on his brother. "What's that supposed to mean?"

"You're afraid to get close to anyone. Afraid they'll hurt you. Afraid they'll let you down. But that's no excuse to keep walking away from everything and everyone."

"I can do whatever the hell I want."

"True, but you'll always be alone if you do."

"Maybe I like being alone."

"And maybe you're full of shit. You're so used to running that you don't know how to stop. I know. I used to do a lot of running myself, always walking away when people got a little close and things got a little too intense. But then Miranda changed all that."

"She made you want to stick around," Brent murmured, remembering the push-pull of emotion he'd felt when he'd stood outside the bathroom door, trying to persuade Abby to open up. He hadn't wanted to leave.

No, for the first time in over one hundred years, he'd wanted to stay put.

"Are you kidding?" Cody smiled. "Miranda made me want to run for my afterlife. Faster, harder than ever before. That's how I knew she was the one. When a woman scares the bejesus out of you like that, she has to be something special." He let the statement hang between them for a long moment before he added, "You should try to talk to Abby."

"I already did that."

"So try again."

"And if she calls the cops?"

"Then you'll figure something out. We'll all figure something out. Together."

The offer was tempting, but Brent had been going it alone, relying on himself, his instincts, his desperation far too long to stop now.

He shook his head. "I can't take that chance. I won't. And if you have half a brain, you won't either. This situation is about to blow up." Then he turned and walked away.

"What about the wedding?" Cody called after him.

"I'm sorry," Brent muttered. And then he climbed into his car, gunned the engine, and left.

16

HE WAS LEAVING.

That's what Brent told himself as he headed down the Interstate. If Cody had any sense of self-preservation, he would follow. But his little brother had gone off the deep end. Home. There was no such thing. There couldn't be. Not for them. They were vampires. Cold. Ruthless.

Scared.

Like hell. Brent wasn't scared. He was smart. He'd learned from his mistakes. It was all about survival. He wasn't running, he was staying alive. There was a difference, even if Cody was too damned lovestruck to see it. He would realize his mistake all too soon and it would be too late.

Not Brent.

He was going to stay one step ahead of the storm.

He was going to stay alive. Even if it meant being alone for the rest of his existence.

Lonely.

The truth struck and the weight of it pressed down on him. He realized then and there that he wasn't half as afraid of being strung up and left to fry in the hot sun as he was of never seeing Abby again.

That thought tore at him far worse than any horsewhip.

He wanted to fall asleep next to her and wake up with her every morning. He wanted her warm body cuddled up next to him and her sweet smile greeting him when he opened his eyes.

Even more, he wanted to pick her brain and find out more about her childhood, her life. He wanted to know and suddenly that thought wasn't half as frightening as the possibility that he might never know. He'd spent his entire afterlife keeping his distance because he thought it would make things easier when it was time to walk away.

It didn't make a bit of difference now. His chest ached and his throat burned.

He was walking away, running away, and it hurt like hell. Far more than anything he'd ever suffered before.

The realization hit him like a two-by-four and his stomach hollowed out. This was his greatest fear.

He wasn't afraid of being discovered. No, he was terrified at the thought of being ripped away from the one thing he wanted most—Abby. And he was doing it himself.

She doesn't want you, buddy.

Maybe not, but he wasn't going to add to the pain by putting more miles between them. She might not want him, but he was going back. He was going to face her and do everything in his power to show her how good they were together.

How good they could be.

And if she freaked and revealed his true identity?

It wouldn't matter. That pain was nothing compared to the thought of never seeing her again. Of giving up. Of not trying.

He hit the nearest Exit and made a U-turn, because Brent Braddock was through walking away.

It was time to stop running and start fighting.

HE WAS KNOCKING on her door again.

Abby listened to the familiar rap of knuckles and fought the urge to jump to her feet, haul open the door and throw her arms around Brent.

He was a vampire.

Even more, he was an annoying, persistent vampire who'd spent the past three days knocking on her door every night.

She hadn't answered, but that hadn't swayed him. She'd half-expected him to kick open the door or morph into a wisp of smoke and slide through the keyhole, but he'd done neither. He'd simply pulled up a chair and talked to her as if they were sitting face-to-face.

He told her about his childhood. About growing up with brothers and horses and lots and lots of cattle. He talked about the war and how he and his brothers had followed Cody to keep an eye on him. And he told her about the massacre and his suspicions that his sister-in-law had been involved somehow.

He told her about his life. And damned if she didn't have the urge to tell him about hers.

She didn't.

She didn't say a word because she knew that even if he'd changed his mind about the two of them getting to know each other, it still didn't make a difference.

It wasn't like they could have a future together.

She had to go back, to clear her name, to keep leading her unit and building her reputation and fighting for what she believed in. She'd worked too hard and sacrificed too much to give it all up to stay in Skull Creek with Brent Braddock.

No matter how much she suddenly wanted to.

So she kept her mouth shut and tried not to hang on his every word. During the day, she prowled the town and tried to keep herself busy. She got her hair done and did more shopping and tried to forget the man waiting back at the motel for her. But none of it was half as much fun as it should have been. Even Winona and her infomercials started to seem depressing. By the time Friday rolled around, Abby had all but given up on reveling in femininity.

Instead, she pulled on an old pair of sweats and a T-shirt and dove into a quart of chocolate ice cream. One more day, she reminded herself. One more day and Rayne would return. Then she would be out of here.

The thought wasn't nearly as comforting as it should have been and she devoured the carton in less than fifteen minutes. She was just reaching for another when she heard his voice.

"I know you love me."

She didn't say a word. She couldn't, due to the sudden lump in her throat.

She couldn't love him. And no way could he love her. They hardly knew each other.

The only trouble with that logic was that she'd gotten to know him over the past few days. Even more, the incredible sex between them had forged a connection. While he couldn't seem to breach her thoughts unless she wanted him to, she could breach his.

She'd discovered that much early this morning while she'd been lying in bed, trying to convince herself to get up and face another long day.

One minute she'd been staring at the ceiling and the next, she'd seen the blaze of fire. Heard the shouts. Smelled the smoke.

She'd seen inside of his head. His nightmare.

She'd felt every lash of the whip as it came down on his back and she'd felt the sting of betrayal. The hopelessness of being surrounded by so much hate. The loneliness of being a one hundred and fifty year old vampire and she'd understood.

Because she'd felt that same loneliness growing up with her father, moving from base to base, never really belonging. But wanting to. Wanting it so badly she could taste it.

The one time she'd taken a chance on easing that want, she'd been devastated.

Like her, Brent had wanted to fit in. To fall in love. To be normal. And so he'd taken a chance too.

And he'd been betrayed. Lila had turned her back on him. Walked away. Run away.

They had much more in common than just the sex.

They were cut from the same cloth, with the same hopes and dreams. The same fears.

"I'm leaving tonight," he said, through the door. "Dillon has a lead on a few women that fit Rose's description. I'm going to fly to New Mexico and check the first one out."

"What about your brother's wedding?" she heard herself ask. "Aren't you going to stay for that?"

"I'm not in much of a mood to celebrate. He'll do fine without me."

"But he's your brother."

"Yeah, well, life's tough. We all learn that sooner or later. I just wanted to let you know." He paused and then she heard the thud of his footsteps as he turned. "I'm sorry about everything."

Before she could stop herself, her hand went to the doorknob. She hauled open the door.

"Brent."

He turned at the sound of her voice. He wore faded jeans, a simple white T-shirt and a relieved expression.

"I know about Lila." She wasn't sure why she told him except that she'd been thinking about it all day. About him. His past. His pain. Her own. She knew he'd been trying to forge a connection with her the past few days and suddenly she wanted him to know that he'd done just that. "I saw her in your dream."

Confusion clouded his face and she wanted so much to reach out. But regardless of the fact that she understood him, that she loved him, she was still leaving. She'd worked too hard to get where she was. She couldn't just abandon it for a man.

Besides, he'd never asked her to. Sure, he'd stuck around but he'd never actually said the words.

Stay with me. Spend the rest of your life with me.

He wouldn't go that far because he was still scared.

"We're connected now. When I close my eyes and clear my head, I can hear what you're thinking. It's the damndest thing." Her gaze met his. "Such is the life of a vampire, right?"

He shook his head. "I don't know what you're talking about."

"I can hear you. In my head. Because we had sex."

"Sex doesn't forge that kind of connection. I've had sex with tons of women and none of them have been able to crawl inside my head. You're the first."

The only.

My one and only.

The truth hung between them for a long moment before he finally turned. "I guess I should get going. I've got a long drive."

Panic rushed through her as he walked away, the feeling growing with his every step. While she knew it was easier to let him leave now instead of later, suddenly she just wanted to seize this moment.

She went after him.

17

BRENT HAD JUST reached his car when he heard Abby's desperate voice.

"Wait."

Her plea crossed the distance to him and he turned.

She reached him a split-second later, her chest heaving, her eyes wild. As if she were about to lose the most important thing in the world to her and she was determined to hold on.

At least for a little while.

"I…" She caught her full bottom lip in her teeth and stared up at him. "Stay with me tonight. One more night. You can leave tomorrow," she added, dashing his hope that she wanted more with him.

A lifetime.

An eternity.

"Why?" If she didn't love him enough to give him forever, he wanted to hear it. He needed to hear it. To give him the strength to refuse her offer.

"Because I want to be with you." She swallowed, her voice small when she finally spoke. "I love you. I know that doesn't change anything, but I needed to say it. I need you to know it." Her hand touched his arm. "Stay with me tonight."

"And tomorrow?" He voiced his biggest fear.

She shrugged. "I don't know. I just know that I don't want you to go."

It wasn't the declaration he'd hoped for, but it was enough for now.

He swept her up and carried her back to the motel room. A sense of urgency rushed through him as he slammed and locked the door and set her on her feet.

Backing her up against the nearest wall, he grasped the hem of her T-shirt. He pulled it up and over her head and tossed it to the hardwood floor. His fingers went to the clasp of her bra and her breasts spilled free.

He dipped his head and drew one sensitive peak into his mouth, relishing the taste and knowing deep in his gut that he could never let her go after tonight.

He wouldn't.

He would fight for this. For her. For them both.

Abby closed her eyes against the wonderful pull of Brent's mouth on her bare breast. He sucked her so hard and so thoroughly, she sagged against him. Wetness flooded the sensitive flesh between her legs and drenched her panties. He drew on her harder, his jaw creating a powerful pull that she felt clear to her core. An echoing throb started in her belly, more intense with every rasp of his tongue, every nibble of his mouth.

The thought faded as she felt the razor-like sharpness against her sensitive flesh. Her body went stiff and he pulled away.

She opened her eyes and found herself staring up at him the way they'd been their last night together. A hot, wild, hungry *vampire*.

He stared down at her, into her, his eyes hot and vivid, his fangs fully visible. He didn't move. Rather, he waited, his body taut, his muscles stretched tight and she knew it took every bit of his strength and then some to hold himself in check.

But he did.

He held back for her, his body trembling with the effort.

She trailed her hand along his jaw, touched his bottom lip and smiled. And then she wrapped her arms around his neck and pulled him flush against her.

He licked at her pulse beat and nibbled as his hand slid into her sweats and between her legs. But he didn't bite her. Not yet.

No matter how much she wanted him to.

Heat flowed through her, pulsing along her nerve endings, heating her body until she felt as if she would explode. His fingers slid inside, plying her soft tissue and stirring the sweetest pressure.

He worked her until she moaned long and low and deep in her throat. Her body throbbed around him. Goosebumps chased up and down her arms. Her legs trembled. Her thighs clenched.

"Please," she murmured.

He plunged his fingers deeper and wetness gushed from her very center. She shivered and cried out.

He caught the sound with his mouth and she felt the sharpness of his fangs against her bottom lip. The sensation sent a ripple of excitement through her.

He pulled her close, his hands trailing down her bare back, stirring every nerve ending along the way. Fingers played at her waistband before slipping lower. His palms cupped her buttocks through the material of her sweats. He urged her up on her tiptoes until her pelvis cradled the massive erection beneath his zipper.

The feel of him sent a burst of longing through her and suddenly she couldn't get close enough, fast enough. She clawed at his T-shirt and wrapped her leg around his thigh. His erection rubbed against her sex and she moaned.

He tugged at the waistband of her sweats and pushed at the material until it slid over her hips, her thighs, to puddle around her ankles. His fingers snagged on the straps of her not-so-sexy panties and urged them down. Until she was completely naked.

He peeled off his shirt and unfastened his jeans. He shoved the denim down in one smooth motion and his erection sprang forward, huge and greedy and swollen. He pushed her onto the mattress, urged her legs apart and settled his erection flush against her.

He slowed down then, kissing her slowly, tenderly for a long moment. Sliding his hands beneath her bottom, he tilted her just so and with one powerful thrust, he slid deep inside.

Pleasure washed over her and forced her eyes closed. Her head fell back and she gave in to the delicious sensation of being filled to the brim with Brent Braddock.

"Open your eyes." His deep voice finally penetrated the desire beating at her temples and she complied.

Hunger blazed hot and intense in his gaze. He opened his mouth. His fangs glittered in the moonlight as he poised above her.

He was giving her one last chance to change her mind. She read the hesitation on his face, felt the hunger clenching his body. She arched her body and tilted her head, baring her neck, offering it to him. Proving beyond a doubt that she accepted him for what he was.

Who he was.

Not just a vampire, but a man.

A man she would never betray.

She wanted his trust. Even more, she wanted this connection with him. She wanted to take all that he offered and give everything back.

She wanted to love him. Completely and thoroughly.

If only for tonight.

He dipped his head. His mouth closed over the side of her neck where her pulse beat a frantic rhythm. He licked the spot, teasing and tasting, and then he opened his jaw wide. His fangs sank deep.

Oddly enough, it didn't hurt. She felt only a sharp prickle, followed by a rush of ecstasy so absolute and intense that it brought tears to her eyes.

But there was more.

He thrust into her, pushing deep with his body all

the while drawing on her with his mouth. The two sensations at the same time, sent her spiraling toward a place where she'd never been before. Higher and higher. The pressure sweeter and sweeter. Until she couldn't take any more. She cried out, splintering into a thousand pieces.

His entire body seemed to vibrate as she came apart. He trembled and buzzed, drinking in her power-infusing blood as he drank in the sexual energy that rushed from her lush body.

His mouth eased and he leaned back.

A fierce groan rumbled from his lips and he plunged deep and followed her over the edge. His body shook and bucked. A frantic heartbeat later, he collapsed atop her, his arms braced on either side of her head, his face buried in the crook of her neck.

His weight pressed her down, a sweet burden that made her chest hitch. She slid her arms around him and held for a few moments, until her heartbeat slowed and he rolled onto his back. He pulled her with him, cradling her close as if he never meant to let her go.

He would.

He was still leaving for New Mexico.

And she was walking away, as well. Rayne was coming home tomorrow and it would all be over. She would drag him back to South Carolina, away from Skull Creek and his new wife.

The thought had never bothered her before, until now.

Until Brent.

But Rayne had made his own bed. He'd run away when he could have easily stayed to face his situation. He could have done things right and returned to the woman he loved an honorable man.

He hadn't and so he had to face the consequences.

It was his fault. At the same time, a spiral of guilt went through her when she thought about breaking the news to his new bride, killing her newfound happiness.

But duty was more important.

Even if it didn't feel that way sometimes.

She ignored the depressing notion and focused on the warmth of Brent's arms. Snuggling deeper, she closed her eyes and tried not to think about tomorrow. Or about the all important fact that she would have to say goodbye.

18

THIS TIME IT WAS Abby who slid from the bed before the crack of dawn.

She tiptoed around the room and snatched up her clothes. Stuffing them into her suitcase, she pulled out the camouflage pants and T-shirt she'd buried her first day in town and dressed quickly. Quietly.

She'd just hoisted her duffel onto her shoulders and grabbed her boots when she spotted the red spandex dress laying on the floor where she'd tossed it all those nights ago. Her chest hitched and she had the insane urge to snatch it up and stuff it into her bag.

For what?

She would never wear it again. The dress had been a part of her fantasy and it was time to wake up now.

To leave.

She cast one last glance at the man sleeping on the bed.

He was sprawled completely naked on top of the covers, his arm flung above his head. Her gaze traveled the length of his body, pausing at all of her favorite spots before she worked her way up and drank in his face, his strong jaw and sensual lips. His lightly stubbled cheeks.

He looked like any other handsome, hunk of a man in the hazy gray that came just before dawn.

A man with needs and wants. Fears and insecurities.

And she was just a woman who felt those same things.

Once upon a time.

It was time to hide that woman away once again and get to work. Rayne was coming home today and while she had no clue when, she did have a hunch where he would go.

She intended to be ready and waiting when he arrived.

Unease niggled at her gut and she double-checked the weapon tucked away in a hidden pocket of her bag. Checking the chamber, she slid the gun into the back waistband of her pants and pulled her shirt down over it. Rayne wouldn't come quietly. Her gut told her that. And so she intended to be prepared for a fight.

She checked the blinds and secured the room against the bright light of day. Leaning over, she kissed Brent Braddock for the last time. She slipped from the motel room, locking the door behind her, and then headed for Rayne Montana's childhood home.

It was time to complete her mission and head back to South Carolina.

If only that thought was half as appealing as it used to be.

SHE WAS GONE.

Brent paced the floor of the motel room an hour later and ignored the exhaustion that tugged at his muscles. It was daylight and he needed to sleep. To rejuvenate.

She was gone. Friggin' gone.

He hadn't meant to fall asleep. But he'd been so tired and she'd been so warm and hell, that's what vampires did in the friggin' morning. They slept.

She'd packed up and hauled ass and he'd been none the wiser.

His gut clenched and awareness sizzled up and down his arms. A strange sensation that he knew all too well. He'd fought too many battles and chased too many outlaws not to recognize the current in the air.

Something bad was going to happen.

And he had no doubt it involved Abby, especially if she was headed to Rayne's old place.

She didn't have a clue what she was walking into. Neither did he, but he had a hunch. He'd tipped off Cody about Abby and he had no doubt that his brother had forewarned Rayne.

He'd hoped that the vampire would have the good sense to just run.

That's what Brent would have done, way back when.

No more. He was here. For better or worse.

He just wished his gut didn't keep telling him it was going to be 'worse'. He snatched up the phone and tried to call Cody, only his brother's voice mail picked up as expected. Cody was dead to the world.

And so was Abby if Brent didn't do something.

She might be able to hold her own in hand-to-hand combat, but Rayne was a vampire. And he wouldn't give up his new bride, his new life, without a fight. Of that Brent was certain.

If Abby had been his wife and they were building a life together, Brent would have fought until his last breath to preserve it and stay with her.

She wasn't. She'd made that painfully clear when she'd walked away this morning.

It was over.

She'd left.

And so they were right back to where they'd started despite what they'd shared last night. Blood and sex and a deeper connection that made him want to bust through the door and go to her.

His gaze went to the tell-tale stain on the pillow, proof that he'd bitten her. His nostrils flared and his mouth watered. He could still taste her. Even more, he could feel her. The determination that drove her. The fear of letting go and getting her heart broken and realizing she was as cold and emotionless as her father. The uncertainty of the future should she fail at the one thing she'd always been good at. The only thing.

They were linked now and as much as that should have bothered him, it didn't.

He loved her. He had from the first moment he'd spotted her at the Dairy Freeze. He'd just been too scared to admit it.

And she loved him.

But it didn't matter. Because she refused to take a chance on that love.

And she was about to walk right into the line of fire.

Rayne would fight. He would kill. Abby, no matter how strong, didn't stand a chance against a determined vampire. She would face off with him, but in the end, he would win.

The truth made Brent pace that much faster, praying for the time to pass quicker so that he could get to her before all hell broke loose.

If only he didn't have the sinking feeling that he was already too late.

SHE WAS WALKING into a trap. The truth struck as she stepped inside the ancient barn and noticed the footprint just in front of her. Just a smudge in the dust that no one else would have noticed except for Abby.

She came to a dead stop.

Her ears tuned to the sounds around her and then it struck her. There were no sounds. No early morning buzz of insects. No birds chirping in the distance. No sizzle of the early morning sun on the frost-covered ground. Nothing.

Just the stillness and the inexplicable feeling that someone was waiting for her.

The barn door slammed shut behind her, plunging the barn into near darkness, and Abby knew her hunch was right.

Someone was already here.

"I see you came back early," she called out, her gaze spanning left and right. "Who tipped you off?" She blinked, adjusting her eyes to the faint light. Only a spiral whispered through the cracks overhead and she wished she'd thought to grab her flashlight.

But then she'd been certain she would be one step ahead of him.

"It doesn't matter. All that matters is that you're here now and you're going back. Jimmy and Mac almost died because of you. Because you just took off and left them without any extra ammunition." She reminded him about their mission. They'd been doing recon, staking out a local militia. She'd taken half the team and circled back to an opposite vantage point. Rayne had followed so that he would know their location. He'd been expected to circle back around. To take extra weapons and join the two they'd left behind. To fight. "You left them there to die."

But they hadn't died.

They'd been captured.

They'd been spotted and attacked, and they'd run out of ammo in the first fifteen minutes trying to defend themselves. "You abandoned them."

"I didn't mean to." Rayne's voice carried from the dark rafters. "I couldn't help it. I couldn't get to them. I was attacked myself."

She had to keep him talking. Then she could

pinpoint his location and get the jump on him. "You were captured?"

"Changed." The voice came from the opposite side of the rafters this time and stopped her cold.

Wait a second.

She whirled, her gaze trained overhead, searching for a glimpse. The hair on the back of her neck prickled and her hand went to the gun she'd stashed in the small of her back.

"I didn't have a choice. I had to leave the unit."

"For Lucy," she reminded him, eager to keep the conversation going. To find him in the darkness. Her interrogation certainly had nothing to do with the fact that she wanted to understand what had happened to him.

"There's no explanation for poor performance." Her father's voice echoed in her head. *"No room for mistakes or excuses."*

"Lucy came later. After what happened outside of Kabul."

"I don't understand."

"I don't expect you would. I'm AWOL and you're worried about covering your ass. It's that simple. You've always been a stickler for following procedure. I had no doubt you would show up here. I just didn't think it would be so quick. I figured you would follow my fake paper trail like the MPs."

"I'm smarter than they are and I know you better."

"Then you know that I'm not going back with you. If you're as smart as you think you are, you'll walk away and forget you ever found me."

"That's not a possibility."

"I don't think you understand." From the corner of her eye, she saw a flash of black and then just like that, he was standing in front of her. "You don't get to make the call on that, chief. I do."

"You *are* going back," she told him. With the flick of her wrist, she pulled the gun free and aimed it at him.

He smiled. "You really don't understand what happened to me, do you?"

She cocked the trigger and held steady. "Should I?"

"Considering you've been shacking up with a vampire for the past few days, I would expect that you might."

The comment sent her reeling, but she didn't so much as blink an eye. She held her hand steady. The gun ready.

Her gaze narrowed. "How do you know about Brent?"

"He's one of us."

His words echoed, followed by his earlier comments.

"Attacked."

"Changed."

"You're a vampire," she murmured as the pieces all fell together and started to fit. "You didn't leave the unit willingly. You were attacked."

"And killed. But then my attacker decided to really punish me by feeding me his blood, so here I am." His gaze met hers and she saw a flicker of the old Rayne. The man who'd fought beside her and had her back for so many years. "I had to leave. I couldn't endanger the team. I didn't understand what had happened to me. I just knew that something was wrong and that I couldn't control it. The hunger was overwhelming. It still is at times, but it's different now. I call the shots. I learned that from Cody."

"Brent's brother?"

Rayne nodded. "My wife is Miranda's sister." He held up his hands and stepped toward her. "I don't want to hurt you, Abby, but I will. I won't leave my wife to go back and face charges for something that wasn't my fault." He took a step forward, but she refused to be intimidated.

She held her ground. "You can explain what happened."

"And end up in a county hospital somewhere,

locked in a padded room? That's not going to happen."

"They won't think you're crazy when they find out there are others like you."

"No, they'll torch the entire town." Determination fired his expression. "I won't endanger my friends. And I won't let you jeopardize everything they've worked so hard to build. This is their home. My home."

"So what are you saying? That you're going to kill me?"

"That you're going to walk away from here and forget all about me." He stared deep into her eyes as if trying to impress his will.

Which was exactly what he wanted to do, she realized.

It didn't work for him any more than it had for Brent. He glared and stepped forward.

"Don't." She held the gun steady. "I'll pull the trigger if I have to."

"No, you won't."

"What makes you so sure?"

"Because I won't let you," came the soft, determined voice directly behind Abby. "I won't let you take my husband and punish him for something he didn't do."

A crack on the head punctuated the sentence.

Abby felt her knees wobble and the ground tremble. And then everything went black.

19

BRENT FELT THE BLOW to the back of his head and he staggered to his knees. The floor shook and for a long moment, his vision clouded.

He had the sudden image of Abby crumpled on the dirt floor and then it disappeared.

His nerves stopped prickling and dread settled in the pit of his stomach.

He forced himself to his feet and walked over to the window. A quick peek and his fingers started to smoke. Pain shot through him, but it was nothing compared to the ache in his chest because he could no longer feel Abby.

The connection had been broken.

She'd been broken.

The realization plagued him as he paced for the

next few hours, waiting and hoping he would feel her again.

Her feelings.

Her thoughts.

Something.

He felt nothing and finally the waiting was too much. His gaze scrambled around the room before focusing on the blanket. He snatched it up, draped it over his head and grabbed his keys.

And then he did the only thing he could think of.

He hauled open the door and went after her.

"I DIDN'T MEAN to hit her that hard." The woman's voice peeled back the layer of sleep that smothered Abby and pounded through her already pounding head.

"You did what you had to do. She had a gun."

"I know. But I don't think she would have used it," the woman insisted.

"You don't know Abby." It was Rayne's voice this time. "She does what she has to do to get the job done. It's reassuring when you're in the field. Not so much when you're holed up in a barn."

"I knew we shouldn't have come here."

"We didn't have a choice. She would have found us eventually. If not here, then somewhere else. It was better we faced her now. We're just lucky Cody was able to warn us."

Silence settled for a few moments before Abby felt a tentative touch at the back of her head. Soft fingers prodded, checking to see the damage that had been done.

"At least there's no bleeding."

"Stop worrying about it. The longer she's out, the bigger a headstart we'll get."

"She's tied up. Even if she comes to, she can't do anything. Speaking of which, maybe we should loosen the ropes a little. I don't want to cut off her circulation."

"You worry too much." Rayne's voice was softer this time and Abby watched through barely closed eyes as he touched his wife's face. "She'll be okay. We'll stash her over behind the hay bales and then we'll get out of here. By the time she wakes up, we'll be long gone."

"Where will we go?"

"I don't know yet, but we'll figure something out. I'm sorry about your school. I know how much Monday meant to you."

"Not half as much as you."

The woman touched her lips to his and for a split second, the world faded. They forgot all about Abby and the fact that her hand was slowly moving toward the knife that sat only a few inches away.

Abby's hand stalled as she watched Rayne hug the voluptuous blonde. Her own chest hitched and she thought about Brent and the fact that she'd walked out on him rather than risk her heart, her career, her life.

This woman had chosen to take the risk. To gamble everything for the man she loved. And here she was, losing everything, yet it didn't seem to matter.

He was all that mattered to her.

And she was all that mattered to him.

Regret knifed at her as she realized that she might never get the chance to take such a risk with Brent. And while that would have been okay a half hour ago, it wasn't now.

Not after seeing two people fight so hard to be together. To stay together.

Abby suddenly wanted to take the risk if it meant having even half of the happiness she saw in front of her.

She shifted her attention to the knife and inched forward. Her fingers had just clasped the handle when Rayne finally noticed.

He flew at her, snatching the knife from her hand and throwing her onto her back. A hiss sizzled in the air and his mouth opened. His fangs pulled back and she knew she'd pissed him off royally. This was it.

The end of the line.

She clamped her eyes shut and braced herself.

But he didn't rip her to shreds. Instead, the barn door crashed open.

In a flash, Rayne flew backwards and Brent leaned over her.

At least she thought it was Brent. Smoke surrounded him, his face red and charred, his hands nearly unrecognizable.

"You're okay," he murmured, his green eyes clouded with pain. But there was something else in them, as well. Relief glimmered, hot and bright, and she knew that he wasn't as destroyed as he looked. "I was so worried about you."

"I'm okay."

"You shouldn't have left—" he started, but the words ended in a fierce groan as Rayne grabbed him by the back of the neck and tossed him to the far side of the building.

Hay scattered and dust smoked. Brent stumbled, stunned for a long moment before he seemed to gather his wits.

With a furious cry, he retaliated and the two vampires went at each other for several moments before a gunshot exploded and cracked open a piece of ceiling.

A circle of sunlight spilled down into the room and both men jumped back out of the burning blaze.

"Stop!" Abby heard her own voice and realized her gun trembled between her bound hands. "Get away from him," she told Rayne who stood dangerously close to Brent.

She aimed the gun at Lucy, intent on making her point. Rayne's eyes flared for a quick second, but then he backed away.

Brent swayed for a few seconds, but then the floor seemed to give way beneath him. He toppled over in a heap of charred flesh and panic rushed through Abby.

"Untie me," she cried, motioning to Lucy. She held the gun at the woman's forehead, determined to do whatever she had to do to get to Brent. The blonde obeyed, working at the ropes for what seemed like an eternity. Finally, Abby was free.

She struggled to her feet, the gun still pointed at Lucy.

"I'll go back with you," Rayne said quietly. "Just don't hurt her."

"I'm not going to hurt her." She tamped down the

fear rushing through her and turned the gun upside down. She handed it over to the blonde, then turned away.

Her gaze riveted on Brent, she rushed toward him.

She dropped to her knees beside him and gathered his limp body in her arms.

"Don't leave me," she murmured, her gaze roaming his body. He was so badly burned that she couldn't imagine him climbing behind the wheel and making it all the way out here, much less surviving. "Please."

It had been the exact plea she'd whispered to Hockey Hunk all those years ago, but this was different. This wasn't the naïve love she'd felt way back when.

This was as real as it could get. She loved Brent. He was her life. Her love. Her man.

She was his woman.

And she wasn't letting him go.

Her eyes blurred then and she blinked, feeling the tears slipping down her cheeks and not caring one way or the other who saw her or whether they thought she was weak.

She was weak compared to Brent.

"I walked out on you. You had no obligation to me. You shouldn't have risked your own neck."

"Sometimes it's worth taking a risk. You're worth it." He gazed up at her, into her and this time she let him.

She didn't put up any fences. She didn't have to. She loved him. And while she'd been hesitant to believe that he really and truly loved her back, there was no doubt in her mind now. He'd braved the sunlight for her.

"I love you," she murmured.

"I know." He touched her face. "I've always known and now so do you." Then he closed his eyes one final time.

20

"DRINK UP."

The deep, familiar voice pushed into Brent's head and lured him back to reality.

He forced his eyes open. His head throbbed and the light hurt his eyes. Even more, his skin felt like he'd been set on fire. Pain gripped him like a vise, clamping tighter, building the pressure and urging him back toward the sweet peace of oblivion.

"Come on, bro. Stay with me long enough to get this down." A hand slid under Brent's aching head and the hard edge of a glass pressed against his cracked and swollen lips.

The first few drops of intoxicating heat touched his tongue and his gut twisted. His skin started to tingle. Then the hunger took control. Whereas he hadn't been able to move a muscle just a moment ago, an instinct as old as time took over and he reached out. His hands reached for the glass and he held on, his mouth open, eager for the sweet salvation drenching his taste buds.

"Easy. You'll make yourself sick drinking the bottled stuff so fast."

"More," Brent groaned when he finished the last drop of the life-renewing liquid.

His head dropped back to the pillow as he waited for Cody to slice open another bag of blood and refill his glass.

He closed his eyes, trying to ignore the pain that beat at his temples. He hadn't had nearly enough sustenance to heal. Rather, he'd consumed the minimal amount to clear the cobwebs fogging his brain.

His heart sped, beating a fast, furious rhythm as he started to think. To remember.

The images started back at the motel. He felt the hardwood floor beneath his feet, the anxiety ripping up and down his spine because Abby had walked away and he couldn't go after her—

"Holy shit." He bolted upright, only to be knocked back down by a rush of pain that gripped every nerve and had him gnashing his teeth.

"Take it easy. It's only been a few hours since Rayne brought you here. You need to heal."

"Where is he?"

"He went home with Lucy once the sun set. Until then, they were stuck in that barn with you. He's okay, but he got a little burned, thanks to the hole in the roof. Now stop talking and have another drink." Cody held up the glass. "This stuff works, but not as well as the real thing. Unfortunately, it's all we have at the moment."

He handed the glass over and Brent took it. He gulped the contents and handed the glass back.

"You need to get some sleep. You'll feel better tomorrow night." Cody went to kill the light, but Brent stopped him.

"I can't sleep." His body tensed and suddenly he needed to move. He forced himself upright, pushing his mangled back up against the wall. The movement felt like he'd taken a sharp knife right between his shoulder blades and he clenched his teeth. A hiss sizzled past his lips.

His gaze skittered around the basement and for the first time, he noted the big screen TV sitting against the far wall. A red bow sat center stage, along with several boxes of surround sound equipment.

"Where did that come from?" he groaned.

"It was a wedding gift from the guys last night. Garret, Dillon and Jake took me to see the bull riding preliminaries over in Travis County to celebrate my last night as a free man."

The party Brent had been responsible for. He'd missed it, just like he'd missed the past one hundred or so years with his little brother because he'd been too busy keeping his distance and staying on the move.

Afraid to get close. To connect.

For fear he'd lose it all over again.

That was the real reason he kept running. He'd had everything way back when and in the blink of an eye, it had been gone. The pain had nearly destroyed him.

So he'd pushed it all away and bricked himself up behind his hard-ass persona, pretending like he didn't care. He'd been at the point that he'd actually stopped caring altogether.

Because it was easier.

But there was nothing easy about the emptiness that sat in the middle of his chest as he stared up and saw the disappointment in Cody's eyes.

"The wedding is tonight." Brent noticed the dark blue slacks and the crisp white shirt his brother wore and he damned himself a thousand times over.

"Three hours and counting." He grinned, but the expression didn't quite touch his eyes. "I hate it that you won't be able to be there, but then, you're not really into weddings anyway."

No, he was into running and keeping his distance and being a bonafide shit.

That's how he felt at the moment. Not just outside, but inside, too.

"Rest up," Cody told him. He set the glass in his hand on the small nightstand and started to turn.

"She's gone, isn't she?" Brent voiced the one question he'd been wanting to ask since he'd first opened his eyes.

"Actually, she's right here." The soft voice crossed the distance to him and his heart lurched.

It couldn't be.

That's what he told himself, but there was no denying the sweet scent of strawberries that filled his head and the frantic heartbeat that echoed in his ears.

His chest hitched and every nerve in his body tensed. He turned. And sure enough, he found Abby standing in the doorway.

"I'll leave you in charge," Cody told Abby, handing her what was left of the bag of blood. "Miranda will kill me if I'm late." Cody ducked out and suddenly it was just the two of them.

"So this is where you've been sleeping when you're not at the motel." Abby swept a glance around the large room. There was very little furniture except for the media stuff sitting in the corner but she had a quick vision of what it would look like with a woman's touch. She couldn't help but smile. "Cody did a good job."

"Yeah," Brent groaned and her heart paused.

He still looked ravaged, but the healing process had already started. His skin still looked red and raw, but it wasn't as disfiguring as it had been before. His hair had started to grow back and she knew by the following day, he would be back to his old self.

Provided he fed, that is.

She reached for the hem of her T-shirt.

"What are you doing?"

"What does it look like I'm doing?" She pulled the cotton up and over her head. She wasn't wearing a bra tonight and the first whisper of air against her nipples brought them to throbbing awareness.

A rush of insecurity welled over her, but she was determined to do this. While she knew he loved her enough to risk everything, she'd yet to be completely open with him. She wanted him to know what he was getting into. And then if he still wanted her, well, they would cross that bridge when they came to it.

"I know I did a pretty risqué striptease the other night," she told him, "but that wasn't really me." She dropped the white cotton to the floor and bent to unlace her boots.

She caught her bottom lip and gathered her courage. "I'm not into fancy clothes or sexy lingerie."

A few frantic tugs of her fingers and she toed off the black monsters. "I've never really been comfortable with all that stuff." She hooked her fingers in the waistband of her camo pants and pushed them down to her ankles. Her panties followed until she was completely naked. "I usually go for fatigues and combat boots. And sometimes I even pick my teeth, but that's beside the point."

"Which is?"

"I'm willing to take a chance on you, on us, but only if you realize what you're getting into. I'm not the kind of woman who freaks out when she sees a spider or waits for a man to open the car door for her. I deal with my own spiders and open my own doors and while I can't say that dressing up was all that bad, for the most part I like to be comfortable. This is me. Take it or leave it."

Brent let his gaze rove over Abby and for the first time, he didn't feel the pain gripping his insides. Instead, he felt frustration. He'd nearly turned himself to dust to protect her and she *still* didn't get it.

Talk about stubborn.

He ground his teeth together and forced himself to his feet despite the flash of panic on her face. Stepping forward, he closed the distance between them until they stood only a few inches apart.

"You look pretty comfortable right now," he pointed out, her nipples rosy and tight.

She glanced down as if only now realizing she'd stripped bare and her cheeks flushed. "I wasn't sure which would help the most. Sex or blood."

"I'm thinking both," he murmured. And then he touched his lips to hers.

21

Both.

The word sparked her memory and pulled her back to the previous night. To his mouth feasting on her neck while his body plunged into hers.

"That's one way to do it." Brent's deep voice pushed into her thoughts and she realized he'd read her mind. Instinctively, she put the wall up, but he shook his head.

"Don't shut me out all the time. It's nice to know what you're thinking once in a while."

She relaxed and stared into his eyes. "So what am I thinking right now?"

"You're wondering if I'm going to bite your neck this time."

"Are you?"

"Maybe." He backed her up against the nearest wall and trailed a finger down her throat.

She swallowed.

"Or maybe I'll try it here." He touched the underside of one breast and traced her ripe nipple. "Then again, I might nibble here." A few tantalizing touches and he slid his palm down, over the soft skin of her abdomen, to the inside of one thigh. "Or here." Her breath caught as he dipped a finger between her legs.

"That would be good." The last word caught as he slipped another finger into her steamy heat and wiggled until a gasp bubbled from her full lips.

"Or maybe I'll try all of them." A hiss worked its way up his throat as he bared his fangs. His body trembled and he touched his mouth to her ripe throat.

She arched her neck, the movement pushing the soft flesh against his fangs and pricking her skin. Her gasp sizzled in the air as a sweet drop of blood bubbled and slid down the luscious curve of her neck.

Brent caught it, relishing the taste before he leaned down to lick the source. A few sweet drops spilled onto his tongue as he laved the prick point clean.

Need twisted inside of him and hunger seized control.

He leaned down and latched onto the ripe tip of her nipple. His fangs sank into the tender flesh of her areola and his groin tightened. Blood spurted into his mouth for a long, delicious moment before he managed to stop himself.

This wasn't just about drinking and healing. It was about branding her as his. Once and for all.

He dropped to his knees and slid his palms around to cup her ass. He gripped her leg and hooked it over his shoulder to tilt her more fully toward him. Then he licked her, tracing the seam of the slick flesh between her legs before he parted her.

She closed her eyes and flattened her palms against the wall, hesitant to touch him because she didn't want to cause him pain.

He knew that because he felt it. He felt her. The pleasure rushing through her and the maddening thought that she was going to die if he didn't take a bite out of her.

Now.

He drew her clit into his mouth and she jumped. He suckled her for a long moment before replacing his lips with his fingers. Shifting his mouth to the tender inside of one thigh, he licked the soft spot. The smell of sex filled his nostrils and fed the already ravenous appetite gripping him. A growl rumbled past his lips. He sank his fangs deep and drew on her.

Convulsions gripped her and her legs gave out, but Brent caught her.

He would always catch her. From this day forward.

A shudder ripped through him as he started to draw on her. Her essence filled his mouth and the tingling energy of her climax zapped him at every point of contact.

But it wasn't enough. He wanted to be inside of her. He needed to be inside of her.

Pulling back, he got to his feet and swept her up. He could feel his strength returning, his body recharging. And while the pain was still there, it faded in the rush of need that gripped him.

He urged her down onto the cot and followed. He skimmed her body, his fingertips brushing her neck, her collarbone, the slope of her breasts, the indentation of her ribs. She was his now and she knew it. And the realization made him all the more desperate for her.

He lowered his head and drew her nipple fully into the moist heat of his mouth.

He suckled her long and deep, until her lips parted and a gasp escaped.

Reaching down, he traced the soft folds between her legs before pushing inside just a fraction. She quivered and he lingered, suckling her breasts, first one then the other.

"I want you," he murmured. "I don't care what you wear or don't wear. I don't care if you get rid of your own spiders or open your own doors or wear a pair of high heels ever again. I want you." He pushed his finger deep to punctuate his statement. "Are we clear?"

"Yes." Abby stared up into his gaze and a rush of joy went through her, because she finally believed him. And she was going nuts thanks to his expert hands. She lifted her pelvis, focusing on the pleasure that gripped her as she worked her body around his decadent finger. She swayed from side to side, her movements frantic, desperate.

"I love you." The words pierced the humming in her ears and she went still. Her eyes opened to find him staring down at her. Waiting.

"I love you, too," she said.

His mouth swooped down and captured hers in a deep kiss that went way beyond anything she'd ever felt before. He coaxed her open and slid his tongue inside and drew on her as if he couldn't get enough. He plundered her mouth with his, exploring and savoring. The air stalled in her lungs and her heart sped faster. A few more seconds, and he tore his mouth from hers.

He slid down her body, now slick from the fever that raged inside of her, leaving a blazing path with the velvet tip of his tongue. With a gentle pressure, he parted her thighs and stroked the soft folds between her legs.

She was wet and throbbing and the discovery made him swear softly. Tremors seized her when she felt his warm breath blowing softly on the inside of her thigh. His tongue darted out, laving the tiny prick points where he'd drunk from her, and it was like being zapped by a live wire. Pleasure crackled through her and she gasped. She clutched at the sheets, desperate to keep her hands to herself since his body had yet to heal completely.

She wasn't sure what happened after that. She only knew that one minute he had his jeans on and the next, he was settling his naked body between her damp thighs.

With a swift thrust of his hips, he impaled her on his rigid length. Sensation overwhelmed her at first. The feel of him so hot and thick pulsing inside her nearly made her come then and there, but then he withdrew and the sensation eased just enough for her to catch her breath.

He slid back in a second time, his hard length rasping her insides and she caught her bottom lip. He kept moving, his body pumping into hers, pushing her higher with each delicious plunge. She lifted her hips, meeting him thrust for thrust, eager to give back as much as he was giving her.

She stared up at him, into the brilliant purple of his gaze and gave herself over to the convulsions that gripped her. He followed her over the edge, a moment later, in a rush of warmth.

They lay in each other's arms for several long moments afterwards, before she leaned up on one elbow and eyed him.

Sure enough, he looked a hundred times better than when she'd first walked into the room. The redness was fading. He was healing.

"Should we do it again?"

He turned his brilliant green gaze on her. "Darlin', we're going to do it so many times, you won't be able to see straight."

"Is that a promise?"

"One I fully intend to keep." He touched his lips to hers in a long, lingering kiss that filled her with such joy she felt her eyes sting. "You don't have to leave the military. I'll follow you anywhere, Abby. I can hire a private investigator to do the legwork and find Rose if I have to."

"You don't have to do that. I understand your need to get to the bottom of what happened."

"Not if it means losing you. I want you to be happy. And if going back makes you happy—"

"I wasn't happy," she cut in, pressing a finger to his lips to silence him. "I was hiding. I threw myself into my career so I wouldn't have to think about everything I was missing. A family. A home. I want both of them, Brent." She shook her head. "I'm not re-enlisting. I'll take the blame for Rayne's MIA and let them force me out with a dishonorable discharge. Then I'll come back here. Or I'll follow you to New Mexico. Or wherever you need to go. We're a team."

"It doesn't seem fair for you to take the blame for Rayne."

"What isn't fair is forcing him to take the blame for something that wasn't his fault. He doesn't deserve that. He deserves a little happiness. We all do." She grinned and eyed him. "What?"

"I never figured you for a hopeless romantic."

"You don't know everything."

"Is that so?"

"You need something to look forward to, otherwise forever is going to be a really long time."

"Not nearly long enough." He leaned down and

caught her in a deep, searing kiss that told her he was feeling much better. "Before we go for round two, there's something I need to do first."

22

AN HOUR LATER, Brent found Cody pacing the back hallway of the Sawyer Ranch as he waited his cue to join the guests and the justice of the peace behind the house where the ceremony was to be held.

Surprise gleamed on Cody's face when he spotted his older brother. "What are you doing here?"

"Being your best man." Brent shrugged on the jacket Miranda had thrust at him the moment he'd driven up with Abby. "If the job's still open, that is."

Cody gave him a questioning glance before his face split into a grin. "I thought you didn't do weddings?"

"This isn't just any wedding. My little brother is getting married for the first time." He caught his brother's gaze. "And the last time."

Cody's smile widened and a warmth spread through Brent.

He flexed his shoulders and, thanks to Abby, felt only a small stinging between his shoulder blades. Her blood flowed through his veins and her thoughts rooted in his head.

"Don't forget the tie."

He pulled the scrap of silk from his pocket and wound it around his neck just as Garret signaled them from the patio doorway.

"It's time."

Brent finished knotting the tie and turned toward his brother. "You ready?"

"I was born ready."

He clapped his brother on the back. "Then let's go get you married, hoss."

* * * * *

COMING NEXT MONTH

Available July 27, 2010

#555 TWICE THE TEMPTATION
Cara Summers
Forbidden Fantasies/Encounters

#556 CLAIMED!
Vicki Lewis Thompson
Sons of Chance

#557 THE RENEGADE
Rhonda Nelson
Men Out of Uniform

#558 THE HEAT IS ON
Jill Shalvis
American Heroes

#559 CATCHING HEAT
Lisa Renee Jones

#560 DOUBLE PLAY
Joanne Rock
The Wrong Bed

REQUEST YOUR FREE BOOKS!

2 FREE NOVELS
PLUS 2
FREE GIFTS!

HARLEQUIN®

Blaze

Red-hot reads!

HARLEQUIN®

A Romance

FOR EVERY MOOD™

Spotlight on

— Heart & Home —

Heartwarming romances
where love can happen
right when you least expect it.

See the next page to enjoy a sneak peek
from Harlequin® American Romance®,
a Heart and Home series.

Five hunky Texas single fathers—five stories from Cathy Gillen Thacker's LONE STAR DADS *miniseries. Here's an excerpt from the latest,* THE MOMMY PROPOSAL *from Harlequin American Romance.*

"I hear you work miracles," Nate Hutchinson drawled. Brooke Mitchell had just stepped into his lavishly appointed office in downtown Fort Worth, Texas.

"Sometimes, I do." Brooke smiled and took the sexy financier's hand in hers, shook it briefly.

"Good." Nate looked her straight in the eye. "Because I'm in need of a home makeover—fast. The son of an old friend is coming to live with me."

She was still tingling from the feel of his warm palm. "Temporarily or permanently?"

"If all goes according to plan, I'll adopt Landry by summer's end."

Brooke had heard the founder of Nate Hutchinson Financial Services was eligible, wealthy and generous to a fault. She hadn't known he was in the market for a family, but she supposed she shouldn't be surprised. But Brooke had figured a man as successful and handsome as Nate would want one the old-fashioned way. *Not that this was any of her business…*

"So what's the child like?" she asked crisply, trying not to think how the marine-blue of Nate's dress shirt deepened the hue of his eyes.

"I don't know." Nate took a seat behind his massive antique mahogany desk. He relaxed against the smooth leather of the chair. "I've never met him."

"Yet you've invited this kid to live with you permanently?"

"It's complicated. But I'm sure it's going to be fine."

Obviously Nate Hutchinson knew as little about teenage

boys as he did about decorating. But that wasn't her problem. Finding a way to do the assignment without getting the least bit emotionally involved was.

Find out how a young boy brings Nate and Brooke together in THE MOMMY PROPOSAL, coming August 2010 from Harlequin American Romance.

THE HEAT IS ON
by
Jill Shalvis

The attraction between Bella and
Detective Madden is undeniable.
But can a few wild encounters
turn into love?

Don't miss this hot read.

*Available in August
where books are sold.*

red-hot reads

HARLEQUIN *Presents*

The Balfour Brides

A powerful dynasty,
eight daughters in disgrace...

Absolute scandal has rocked the core of the infamous
Balfour family. The glittering, gorgeous daughters are in
disgrace.... Banished from the Balfour mansion, they're
sent to the boldest, most magnificent men
to be wedded, bedded...and tamed!

And so begins a scandalous saga of dazzling glamour
and passionate surrender.

Beginning August 2010

MIA AND THE POWERFUL GREEK—*Michelle Reid*
KAT AND THE DAREDEVIL SPANIARD—*Sharon Kendrick*
EMILY AND THE NOTORIOUS PRINCE—*India Grey*
SOPHIE AND THE SCORCHING SICILIAN—*Kim Lawrence*
ZOE AND THE TORMENTED TYCOON—*Kate Hewitt*
ANNIE AND THE RED-HOT ITALIAN—*Carol Mortimer*
BELLA AND THE MERCILESS SHEIKH—*Sarah Morgan*
OLIVIA AND THE BILLIONAIRE CATTLE KING—*Margaret Way*

8 volumes to collect and treasure!
